"Captain [...] your servi[...]

Becky licked [...] sinful tongue [...] look that made his entire body lurch.

"I've never seen you in uniform before," she said. "You wear it well." She scanned him from shoulder to shoulder, from head to toe. "Take it off, Captain."

In a single beat of time, the atmosphere in the room thickened.

"The hotel cleaners just sent it up, starched and pressed," he tried to argue.

"So we'll make it a point not to wrinkle it," she said, grinning wickedly. "Come on, soldier. Take it off and come over here." Becky reached for the knot of terry cloth between her breasts and dropped her towel.

She was naked.

Damn. Zachariah's penis throbbed to shameless attention as he stood, transfixed, by all her abundant glory. His body knew he was fighting a losing battle. He might as well go with it.

"At your command…"

Dear Reader,

It's hard to believe that *At Your Command* is my thirtieth book! Many of my stories are still so fresh in my mind that it feels as though I could find a town on a map, walk up to a door, knock – and one of my characters would answer.

At Your Command features one such character, a man who jumped off the pages. Captain Zachariah Clark was Travis's e-mail buddy in my Mills & Boon® Blaze® novel, *Basic Training*. By the time we met him in person in that story, Clarksie had created a rather large presence for himself. Now this big, sexy marine has come home after serving in a war zone. But his reunion with a wife he barely knows may not go as smoothly as he hopes. Being apart for eighteen months is hard. But sometimes, coming home can be even harder.

Do you have a favourite fictional character you'd like to meet in person? I've always thought hanging out with Miss Marple or Atticus Finch would be cool. You can visit me online at www.juliemiller.org and share your thoughts.

Enjoy,

Julie Miller

AT YOUR COMMAND

BY
JULIE MILLER

MILLS & BOON

Pure reading pleasure

First published in Great Britain 2009
by Harlequin Mills & Boon Limited,
Eton House, 18-24 Paradise Road, Richmond, Surrey TW9 1SR

© Julie Miller 2008

ISBN: 978 0 263 87483 9

14-0609

Harlequin Mills & Boon policy is to use papers that are
natural, renewable and recyclable products and made from
wood grown in sustainable forests. The logging and
manufacturing processes conform to the legal environmental
regulations of the country of origin.

Printed and bound in Spain
by Litografia Rosés S.A., Barcelona

JULIE MILLER

is an award-winning author – with a National Readers Choice Award, a Daphne du Maurier Award and a PRISM Award, among other prizes. She's been a finalist in several other venues, including the Golden Heart contest. She has been a multiple nominee for *Romantic Times BOOKreviews* awards, including Best Blaze®, Best Contemporary Paranormal and *Romantic Times BOOKreviews'* Career Achievement Award for Series Romantic Suspense. Some of her thirty-plus books have appeared on the *USA TODAY* and Waldenbooks bestseller lists. Born in Missouri and now living in Nebraska, Julie gets support from her small but mighty writing group, the Prairieland Romance Writers, as well as her husband, son and smiling guard dog, Maxie. Find out more about the author at www.juliemiller.org. You can e-mail her through her website or write to her at PO Box 5162, Grand Island, NE 68802-5162, USA.

For my Mizzou buddy, Jas.

I remember brainstorming behind the dorm (while we sunned ourselves without a thought about skin cancer and wrinkles…er, pardon me, laugh lines!) to create wonderful stories that I wrote in all my notebooks. Eventually I took bits and pieces of those ideas and put them into my computer years later when I decided to seriously pursue this writing thing. You didn't think I was crazy for having such an imagination – instead, you joined in the adventure with me. You even gave me a "writing kit," full of paper and folders, properly marked with all my working titles. I still have it.

What support. What encouragement.

What a friend.

1

Eighteen months ago

MARINE CORPS CAPTAIN Zachariah Clark was so tuckered out he could barely put on his uniform, much less speed up the process.

But, oh, man, what a way to go.

He had only five hours until he had to report for duty at the training base in Quantico, Virginia—forty miles away. Against city traffic. Through the mushy dregs of the snowstorm that had blanketed Washington, D.C. He should be kickin' his ass into gear and bookin' it out of this hotel.

But as he tied off his boots, all he could think about was the naked woman in the shower, singing a bluesy rendition of "Too Darn Hot" that danced against his eardrums like a seductive whisper and heated his groin like the touch of a slow, firm hand.

"Keep dressin', Clarksie," he chided himself as he carefully buttoned the fly of his camouflage pants.

After nearly a week in this room with Becky Owens, he thought he would have gotten the woman out of his system. He'd already had her six ways to Sunday, and she'd had him back.

Enough, man! Duty calls.

But she was in there.

Naked.

Absolutely his favorite version of the Beckster. He'd seen her in every role from buttoned-up exec in a chaste gray suit to adorable sex kitten in her funky flannel pajamas. He'd had fun with them all. But naked? He swallowed hard, doing his damnedest to blank out the image of soft, decadent curves, flexing and bouncing with each precise movement she made. The pale, perfect skin, the result of her Scandinavian heritage, would be steaming beneath the spray of the water.

Naked.

Zachariah reached for the khaki T-shirt he'd pulled from his duffel bag. Maybe if he kept puttin' his clothes on, he'd quit obsessing about takin' hers off.

Of course, he wouldn't have to take off anything because she was already…

Naked.

Shit. His dick stirred in response.

"Helluva pep talk, Clarksie."

He pulled the T-shirt over his head, stretching the cotton over his chest and arms until the Corps tattoo of eagle, globe and anchor peeked out beneath the sleeve on his left bicep. Yeah. Focus on that. Think Semper Fi. Think duty. Honor. His responsibility to his men and country. Neutralizing threats around the world. An eleven-year career.

Naked.

"Geez."

Zachariah's pants tightened.

He resolutely tucked in his T and pulled his camo overshirt off its hanger as Becky's husky serenade ended. The pulse of beating water dwindled to a few noisy drips and then silence. Lordy. If she walked out here naked…

Zachariah inhaled a deep, steadying breath and buttoned his shirt. He was a Marine, damn it, not some lovesick puppy. Though, with his mug, he hadn't had the same success as some of his poster-boy comrades; this wasn't the first time he'd come home on leave, picked up a woman at a bar and spent the night with her. It was the first time he'd spent *six* nights with the same woman. The first time he'd ever had any trouble kissing her goodbye, thanking her and walking away.

Hell. He was beginning to feel like he was never going to get enough of her. The cool, conservative attorney with the secretly sinful alter ego wasn't intimidated by his crew cut or brawn or bad-ass bravado. If anything, the challenge of going head-to-head with him seemed to excite her. It excited him. From the moment she'd walked into Groucho's Pub in the heart of D.C. nearly a week ago, and refused to let him buy her a drink, the game between them had been on.

How could he leave before the game was finished?

The bathroom door creaked open.

Despite his best, self-preserving intentions, Zachariah's gaze searched the mirror over the hotel room desk where he was dressing. He zeroed in on the cloud of steam filtering into the archway behind him, a tempting prelude to the Venus who'd follow.

The steam carried the exotic scent that was uniquely

Becky's—a heady fragrance that reminded him of long nights in the tropics. Everything in him tensed with anticipation. If she was naked…

"Whew! Now I'm awake." The steam cleared and Becky appeared in the doorway.

Thank God. He'd be able to walk away.

Maybe.

She wore a white, fluffy towel, tucked around her breasts sarong-style, covering her from her armpits to her thighs. It was a demure enough look if he didn't already know what was hidden underneath. The skin he could see was pink from the shower's heat, and try as he might, he couldn't look away from the tempting sight. She dried her hair with a second towel, then tossed it onto the marble vanity beside the bathroom sink.

Zachariah dropped his gaze to the glimpse of rounded butt cheek that appeared beneath the edge of the terry cloth as she leaned in closer to the mirror running the length of the vanity. He glanced back up as she finger-combed her hair. Damp from her shower, the white-gold waves had darkened to the color of wheat. One tendril stuck to her cheek, and before Zachariah could even identify the urge to do the job for her, she pulled it free and tucked it behind her ear. Only then did her deep cobalt eyes look up to meet his reflection in the mirror. "Good morning, big guy."

I have to go, he meant to say.

"God, you're gorgeous," he said instead. *That's tellin' her, Clarksie. Way to be large and in charge.* How the hell was he supposed to begin this farewell conversation? Where was that hoo-yah drive to get the job done?

Twin dots of rosy color dotted her creamy cheeks—the ones up top. But she neither thanked him for the compliment nor made any effort to put him out of his ineloquent misery. Instead, Becky pulled a bottle from her toiletry bag and dabbed lotion onto her face. She worked and conversed as if this was any other morning. As if they had a thousand more mornings together instead of just hours.

"You wore me out last night. Again." Her low, husky laugh danced across his skin. His dick stirred in a helpless response to the sound, as if she had caressed him there. "I don't think I've ever had this much exercise on a vacation before."

Setting aside his goodbye mission for a moment, Zachariah played the double-entendre game, too. "I've always enjoyed a good workout myself."

"So…" She eyed his duffel bag on the bed. "Where will you be?"

The bantering mood broken, he returned his attention to adjusting his collar. "We talked about this last night."

"I know you have to return to base to report for duty by noon—1200 hours, you said. I meant, where will you be stationed after that?"

She wasn't game-playing. But he couldn't give her the straight answer she wanted. "That information's classified."

Pulling out a comb, she made a job out of smoothing her hair into a sleek style before it dried into the loose tumble of waves he preferred. "Do we try to keep in touch? Write letters? Will you have access to a phone or e-mail?"

"Possibly. But I'd have to contact you first to let you know the when, where and how. Until then, you won't be able to reach me."

She nodded. "Will your mission be dangerous?"

Special Ops assignments always were. He wasn't an idiot about his safety or the safety of his men, but the risk inherent in his work couldn't be denied. "Yes."

"Are you headed to the Middle East?"

"Can't say."

"Africa?"

"Classified, darlin'."

"Are you staying stateside? Fighting the war on drugs?"

"I can't tell you."

Becky huffed what sounded like a curse, tossed the comb into the sink and spun around. "What *can* you tell me?"

Was it the lawyer in her, asking all these questions? Was she picking a fight to make sure there weren't any lingering emotions or foolish expectations once he walked out the door? Or was this how she masked her concern? Sometimes, his parents got funny, too, over how secretive his work could be.

"I'm waiting." She gripped the vanity on either side of her, thrusting her tits forward in a defiant posture that strained the confines of the towel.

Zachariah carefully considered her request. Even the Corps couldn't control the way a man felt—but regulations were regulations. He held his hands up in mock surrender. "I can say that you may well have *the* most perfect set of breasts on the planet. Big enough that they can fill these hands without feelin' like I'm gonna break something, yet soft and sassy enough that I know I'm dealin' with the real thing."

After a long pause, the stern lines around her mouth eased and she laughed. "You like these, hmm?"

"Oh, yeah." Zachariah's own mouth shifted into a cautious smile. "Are we okay?"

She nodded. "It's been fun, hasn't it? Certainly not how I was expecting to spend these last few days before starting my new job with the State."

"Not what I had planned for my leave, either. But yeah, it was—" though the word felt inadequate, Zachariah felt stymied to come up with something better "—fun."

"And you're leaving in five hours?"

He'd better leave now. Or he'd have a unit of MPs on his tail to haul him back to base. Despite the desire drumming through his body, and the longing and guilt twisting him up deeper inside, Zachariah gathered his keys and billfold and stuffed them into his pockets. "I have to be at Quantico in five hours. I'm leaving sooner than that." He picked up his duffel, but paused when he noted how her face had gone pale. This was what military life was like. She had to understand that. "I told you when this started it was gonna be short and sweet between us."

"And I agreed to that. I have a new job to focus on. I'm fixing up my own place. I'm not looking to invest in a long-term relationship." She pulled her lush bottom lip between her teeth as she slipped into deep thought. Zachariah fought to get past the need to taste that sweet lip himself, and listened to what she had to say. "Saying goodbye is tougher than I expected."

"Yeah." *Wow. That was profound, buddy.* He thumbed over his shoulder toward the door. "I need to go."

Becky released her lip and straightened. She'd checked whatever emotion she'd been feeling, and now he could see the wheels churning behind those deep blue eyes. Zachariah braced himself to deal with whatever she was thinking up. "How long does it actually take you to get to the base from here?"

"About an hour. Unless I hit some freaky midmorning traffic out of D.C."

Her lips curved into a serene smile. "I just realized—I've never seen you in uniform before."

Pulling his shoulders back, Zachariah proudly gave her a good look at what 280 pounds of big, bad Marine looked like. "Captain Zachariah Clark at your service, ma'am."

Becky lapped her sweet, pink tongue around her lips in an assessing, appreciative pout that made his entire body lurch. "You wear it well."

"Thanks."

She scanned him from shoulder to shoulder, from head to toe. Then she looked him straight in the eye. "Take it off, Captain."

"Becky—"

"I said take it off."

In a single beat of time, the atmosphere in the room had thickened.

"The hotel cleaners just sent it up, starched and pressed."

"So we'll make a point not to wrinkle it." She reached for the knot of terry cloth between her breasts and dropped her towel.

Naked.

Damn. Zachariah's cock throbbed to shameless attention as he stood transfixed by all her abundant glory.

"Take it off. And get over here."

Zachariah tossed the duffel onto the bed. "At your command."

He stripped in record time, never even considering the bed as he swapped his uniform for their box of condoms, and strode across the room with a single purpose. Her.

Becky's kiss was waiting for him as he lifted her up onto the bathroom counter and spread her legs to move between them. She smoothed the friction between their lips with her tongue, then delved inside to toy with his. Every stroke kicked up the heat throbbing through him another impossible notch. She linked her arms behind his neck and pulled herself up against his body, teasing his chest with the brush of her nipples, teasing him down below with her fragrant, dampening heat. She was a decadent delight for each of his senses—from the contrasting reflection in the mirror of his suntanned hands moving over her fairer skin to the minty taste of her bold tongue in his mouth.

Zachariah tried to savor every moment, taking note of every sensation so he could replay the memories months from now when he was stuck in the middle of the desert or in some foreign jungle—far from letters and e-mails, farther still from kisses and touches like these.

But patience wasn't his friend this morning.
Becky's mouth was pliant and eager, matching every
foray he made. She trailed her fingers along his spine,
sparking an electric impulse in every cell she touched.
Still anchoring her atop the counter, Zachariah slipped
his hand down between them, seeking her heat, testing
her readiness. He stroked one finger along her slick
crevice and she gasped, tearing her mouth from his and
burying her face against his neck.

"Mmm."

An answering groan from deep in his chest was all
he could manage. He dipped one finger inside her,
then two. She writhed against his hand. He found her
responsive nub with his thumb and begged the cool,
calm, controlled attorney to go wanton on him.

"Not fair," she gasped, nipping at his collarbone.
"You have to—" her hum vibrated against his skin
"—come…too." Her knees flexed convulsively around
his hips as she neared her release. He knew the feeling.
Understood the need. His aching dick poked her hip
and thigh as he rocked helplessly against her. Zachariah was like a temperature trigger on a brick of C-4
explosive, rapidly heating up to the point of detonation.

Becky's fingers dug into his back. "Zachariah?"
She was breathing hard. "Zacha—" breathing deeply
"—Zachari…?" Breathing quickly.

After seven days together, he recognized the sound.
She was coming.

So was he.

"Not yet." She kissed his neck. Kissed his chin.
Grabbed his wrist and pulled his slick fingers from her

before she climaxed. "Together," she demanded. "This last time, we do it together."

Their fingers tangled as they reached for the condoms he'd dropped beside her. There was laughter. Kisses. Fumbling hands.

"Enough." He issued the order before he embarrassed himself right there on the counter. Taking charge of the race to their completion, he ripped open a package and turned his back on her to sheathe himself.

Not to be left out of the action for even a moment, she kissed his shoulder blade and reached around to tease his nipples into tortuous attention. "Beckster…" He groaned the warning, then went back on the offensive.

They were damn well going to finish this together. Zachariah turned and pulled her to the edge of the counter. She was more than a foot shorter than him. But tall enough that she was aligned perfectly with his straining, needy self. He pushed her thighs apart and nudged her entrance.

Wanton, indeed. With her hands clutching his biceps for balance, she arched her neck, thrusting her breasts up like an offering, her luscious globes bobbing beneath his hungry gaze. He studied the delicate red and blue veins engorging the hard tips, then squeezed one in his big hand and dipped his head to suckle her. Becky bucked against him as he pulled harder and harder. "Please. Please."

He didn't want to leave her. His conscience said he couldn't just walk. They'd been pretty careful. But they'd also been pretty wild. Pretty intense. Pretty…frequent.

What if her pill or his condom had failed?

What if he came back and she'd moved on to someone else?

Couldn't happen.

Wouldn't happen.

"Zachariah…" she commanded, linking her heels behind his thighs and opening herself even wider. "Take me. Now."

The order alone was enough to send him right to the edge.

Pinpricks of light danced behind his eyes as the inevitable countdown toward detonation began. "Marry me."

"What?"

He slid his tip inside, barely an inch—denying for a moment what they both craved. They were breathing hard as he held himself on the brink and looked down into her blue eyes, locked onto his. The wheels were again spinning inside her head, evaluating the timing and motivations behind his impulsive—yet surprisingly serious—request.

"Don't let this end. Marry me."

His body nearly spasmed as he refused to indulge his need until she gave him an answer.

"Okay."

"Okay?"

Becky grabbed his ass and urged him in. With one deep thrust, Zachariah exploded inside her. She shattered around him and cried out, "Yes!"

2

"ZACHARIAH! HEY, BIG GUY! Welcome home!"

Becky snatched her hand out of the air and pulled it into a fist near her stomach, mortified by her blind enthusiasm. Thank God the crowd of families and friends surrounding her had cheered loudly enough to drown out her impulsive shout. Glancing quickly around, she wished she were tall enough to see over more of the men and women near her.

"Smooth one, Owens," she muttered under her breath.

Had she flagged anyone's attention? Not that she'd really expected her least favorite fan to follow her the eighty miles from Richmond, Virginia, to the Marine Corps base at Quantico. He hadn't had the balls to use his own phone or leave a name or traceable address yet, so she doubted he'd really show his face. But the letters and phone calls—no doubt the vengeful enterprise of one of the ex-husbands she'd pursued on behalf of her clients—were coming more frequently now. And dead roses had been left on the windshield of her car and at the front door to her condo, kicking the anonymous stalking up another notch.

It started simply with *I hate you* clipped from

random magazine letters and sent to her office, along
with some heavy breathing on her phone at home.
Then he had tried to show he was smart by switching
to computer printouts and adding some big words: *I bet
you aren't getting any, Princess Plump-ass, so you
have to emasculate every man you meet to compensate.*
The latest note, delivered to her office five days ago
with an illegible postmark, had contained a new twist
on the usual insults and hurtful words: *You think you're
all that, don't you, bitch? I'm going to take back what
you've stolen from me. Even if it has to come out of
your hide.* Included had been a photograph of her
walking down the courthouse steps, taken from a
distance. In the picture, her heart had been cut out.

Though she'd reported that last message to her
supervisor at the State Attorney's office, and the letter
and photo had been subsequently filed with the
Richmond PD, there was little they could do beyond
monitoring the situation and working on identifying
the culprit. It wasn't as if Becky didn't have plenty of
candidates to choose from. With her work—taking
deadbeat exes to court on behalf of those who couldn't
afford legal representation—she could name a dozen
suspects who were less than thrilled by the settlements
she'd won. Garnishment of wages. Termination or
alteration of custody agreements. In one case, impri-
sonment. Of course, there was the whole public-
humiliation factor of being exposed as a user or loser,
in addition to the financial costs. Becky was good at
her job. Damn good. Half-assed had never been the
Owens way.

Still, though she'd like to think that someone was mouthing off because he'd gotten his wallet or pride hurt and that the need to strike back would eventually flicker and die, a smart woman wouldn't take any chances. Becky breathed in deeply and curled her fingers through the chain-link fence blocking off the parking lot in front of her. She needed to purge the moment of panic and gather her wits.

Catching a glimpse of a pair of shoulders filling a bus window so completely that she could barely make out the square jaw and light-brown hair above them should not have her squealing like a schoolgirl who'd just been winked at by the senior boy on whom she had a crush. So what if Zachariah Clark's impressive body and effortless strength had plagued her most erotic dreams these past eighteen months?

Eighteen months since she'd thrown Owens expectations to the wind and done exactly what she wanted.

She'd defied her father in order to land a job that allowed her to actually make a difference in the world.

She'd shared a blistering affair with a man she'd met in a bar—an unpedigreed soldier who worked with his hands instead of his family's money.

She'd married him.

Becky exhaled that deep breath between tightly compressed lips. Her conscience had been paying a heavy price for her impetuousness ever since. She wasn't sure she could handle it if her mother or father, or any one of her clients, got hurt because she was distracted and failed to live up to her promises. Their safety and well-being came first. That stalker toad and her own desires had to come in at a self-disciplined second.

She couldn't allow a man's being in her life again to give her a false sense of security, either. Zachariah wouldn't be around for long. And people were depending on *her,* not him. She'd dealt with her problems while he was overseas, and she'd deal with them again after he was gone.

Cool, calm and collected was also the Owens way.

Ha! So why was she standing on tiptoe, trying to steal another glimpse through the windows of the approaching bus? Catching herself, Becky lowered her heels into her Italian leather sandals.

"You don't do *giddy,*" she reminded herself on a muttered breath. She glanced from side to side once more, seeing nothing but eager children and anxious spouses and parents.

Nothing to fear.

No one who seemed interested in her at all.

She forced an angry breath from her lungs, hating that she'd given in to any degree of paranoia. She was here alone. Period. Get over it.

She focused her attention back on the bus.

As the only child of power broker Bertram Owens, "society"—meaning politicos in Richmond and D.C., the family tree and Bertram himself—demanded a certain degree of decorum from her. Whatever spontaneity that hadn't been bred out of her by birth had been thoroughly reined in by years of training—except for six-and-a-half fabulous days with one certain Marine.

In the courtroom and at home, the restraint that she

exercised almost daily served her well. She needed it now more than ever, knowing her father was home at the family estate outside of Richmond, waiting for her to fail. Waiting to pick up the pieces of what he considered her misguided adventure into independent living. Waiting to give her an I-told-you-so, let-me-take-care-of-this-for-you hug and steer her back onto the path an Owens heiress should be taking toward securing the family's future. Namely, marrying one of the stuffy, upper-crust bores on her parents' list of approved suitors, and settling down to expand the family dynasty like a good little girl.

Claiming she was seeing someone—who conveniently traveled a lot outside of the country so she wouldn't have to produce him for family dinners or political receptions—had temporarily staved off her father's obsession with marrying her off to make mergers and grandbabies. If push came to shove, she'd even pull out the marriage certificate. Though the deception would hurt at first, it was just the sort of crafty business maneuver her father might eventually respect.

However, Becky intended to save that revelation as an absolute last resort. Her mother, Lily, was still recovering from chemo and radiation treatments to forestall any recurrence of the breast cancer she'd conquered a year ago. Causing her mom stress by ruining her dreams for her only offspring wasn't particularly appealing. And pissing off Bertram Owens wasn't something that anyone—even his own daughter—did lightly.

It certainly wasn't fair to Zachariah to thrust him

into the midst of the secrets and lies that had become Becky's life this past year.

In D.C., his proposal had seemed like the perfect out to get her father off her back about settling down with the right young man. Plus, she'd fallen victim to the foolish idea that saying yes would somehow prolong the wild and crazy freedom of their week together.

But then her mother's condition had worsened. To be on hand for his wife's treatment and recovery, Becky's father had left his advisory appointment in Washington and moved back to Richmond full-time, working as a political consultant and party fund-raiser. Now he was close enough to check on Becky every day. *Joy.* In person if he wanted. *Rapture.* He played buddy-buddy with her superiors in the State Attorney's office more often than she lunched with her girlfriends. She was a twenty-eight-year-old woman, for gosh sakes!

As much as she loved her parents, Becky refused to surrender her independence. She understood her father's need to control and protect was rooted in love. She understood her mother's dreams were equally altruistic. But Becky wanted to live, thrive—succeed—on her terms. She'd find a way to be her own person, a crackerjack attorney—and the Owenses' daughter.

But none of it was easy.

Zachariah deserved to know what he was really getting into as her husband—what he probably wouldn't want to get into if he *did* know.

And he should hear it from her—face-to-face.

But one look at those tanklike shoulders and her hormones had overridden every sensible intention.

Swamped by emotions, she'd gotten carried away by the cheering crowd. There was something uniquely inspiring and heartwarming about welcoming home a busload of Marines returning from a war zone. Flags were flying. A band was playing. Her patriotism had kicked in, that was all.

She didn't really expect that falling into Zachariah's arms would make all her stresses go away. Not even for the night or two they'd have together.

Zachariah Clark was a man, not a myth. He was a good time. Okay, a very good time.

Be honest, girl.

He was the best time she'd ever had.

But he was a fallback plan, a welcome chapter in her life—not the whole book. He was a Marine who'd left her to do his job while she stayed at home and did hers. She suspected he was damn good at that job, or he wouldn't be given assignments about which she knew so little and he told her even less. But he wasn't a superhero. Okay, so Captain Clark might be built along superhuman proportions, but he was still just a man.

Becky breathed deeply—in through her nose, out through her mouth—steeling herself the same way she did each time she stepped up to argue a case before a judge. She could handle this. She could handle him.

That was the Owens way.

The bus pulled to a stop, and the liaison officer signaled the waiting families to enter through the gate onto the parking lot. But as the crowd carried Becky forward, an anxious anticipation buzzed across her

skin, raising goose bumps. Despite her resolve to keep
this reunion at arm's length and impersonal until she
could explain her situation and determine how Zachariah would fit into her life while he was home on leave,
Becky found herself hurrying right along with
everyone else, trying to spot him the instant he filed
off the bus.

Was he as tall as she remembered? Had he been
injured in any way? Would he still overlook the extra
pounds that stress and genetics wouldn't let her lose,
and show that same lusty desire for her in his eyes?

Oh, my. Becky's breath caught in her chest. *Zachariah.*

He was leaner and more tanned than she recalled.
Harder somehow, through the squint of her eyes.
Still, Zachariah Clark was impossible to miss.
Standing a head taller than most of his comrades, he
stepped off the bus with a wary alertness, already
scanning the crowd.

"Zachariah!" *Damn.* Her hand shot into the air again
and she waved.

Play it cool, Owens. Play it cool.

But his green eyes had already zeroed in on her.
They widened with recognition. His rugged features
softened with a lopsided grin. "Beckster!"

Screw decorum. Becky ran to greet him.

The people between them parted for those broad
shoulders and captain's bars as Zachariah pushed his
way through the crowd. She met him halfway. He
dropped his duffel bag, and his long, strong arms
snaked around her as she leaped. He caught her and

swung her around, squeezing her tightly and waking every feminine cell inside her with an instant reminder of just how powerfully built and masculine he was. His mouth crushed down over hers long before the world stopped spinning and her toes touched the asphalt beneath her again.

Who was she kidding? She wanted this. Talking could wait. Becky wound her arms around his neck and held on, kissing him, consuming him with a hunger that hadn't abated one whit since D.C. She inhaled his clean, undoctored scent. Absorbed his heat. Clung to his hard strength. Reveled in the evidence of his desire for her, unabashedly swelling against her thigh.

Rational thought fled as embracing Zachariah reminded her how uncomplicated *this* was between them. Parts of her body that had lain dormant for eighteen long months roared to life with a frenzy that shook the Owens family tree. Her blood thickened and pulsed. Her breasts tingled with excitement. She lost track of the crowd, of curious eyes, of unpleasant realities—of everything except the desire to burrow beneath this soldier's starched exterior and wrap herself up in the raw, sensual man inside the uniform.

She was still reaching for another kiss when his mouth withdrew beyond her reach. Zachariah had come to his senses sooner than she had. With his hands massaging circles at her waist, Becky braced her palms against the ragged rise and fall of his chest and tried to recover her own breath. "Wow."

Bending to touch his forehead to hers, Zachariah's eyes sparkled with amusement. "Now *that's* what I call a welcome home."

Beaming beneath the approval in his low, rumbly voice, Becky twisted her fingers beneath his collar. "You haven't seen half of what I've got planned for you this weekend, soldier."

"It's *Marine,* darlin'." He pulled her hips forward into his, reminding her that he was ready for action. "But as long as you've made plans, I won't quibble over…"

He angled his face as if he intended to kiss her again. But he jerked back, halfway to his destination, leaving her lips puckered with anticipation. His grip pinched hard at her waist and her mouth rounded into a startled, "Ow!"

Becky twisted, trying to free herself. He'd never hurt her before. Not once. Not even in fun. So what was the deal?

"Zach…" But her protest died at the face frozen above her. Staring straight over the top of her head. Her own warning jets fired and she quickly glanced behind her. "What is it?"

Families. Marines. Flags. Laughing. Crying. Hugging. Nothing weird.

No one watching.

Becky turned back to the blankness chilling his eyes. "Big guy?"

Grooves deepened beside his eyes and mouth, twisting his features into a frown. His nostrils flared with a deep, stuttering breath. What was happening here?

Becky skipped curiosity and moved straight to

concern. She nudged at his chest, then reached up and caught his jaw between her hands, giving him a little shake. She uttered his name with more force. "Zachariah!"

He blinked and his eyes blazed back into focus so suddenly she thought she might have imagined the whole weird disconnect.

Except Becky Owens wasn't given to idle imaginings. "Where did you go?"

He shook his head as if confused by her question. "I'm right here."

"A second ago, you were a million miles away."

"Fatigue, I guess." Zachariah seized her wrists and pulled her hands from his face. "I'm pretty wiped out, adjusting to the time differences and all."

"Are you sure? It seemed like more than that."

If it weren't for the almost tentative restraint in his normally confident touch, she might have believed the cocky grin that slid back into place. "It's good to see you again," he said, without explaining anything to her satisfaction. "And to touch you." He brushed the tip of her nose with his finger.

Okay. Nose tapping aside, she'd go along with the diversionary tactic instead of following up with a more probing question. After all, she couldn't very well force the husband she barely knew to unburden his secrets to her if she wasn't ready to do the same for him.

But she could care. She *did* care. Putting her desires on the back burner, Becky slid her arms around his waist. She walked into his chest and hugged him tightly, offering him something a little calmer, a little saner than the healthy lust that zinged like perpetual lightning between them.

After a moment's hesitation, Zachariah folded his arms around her shoulders and hugged her back. "Hey. What's this for?"

She turned her nose into the crisp, starched scent of his uniform. "I'm sorry I wasn't a better letter writer, and that I didn't e-mail you more often. I'm sorry I'm not a better…" Oh, crud. The word was sticking to her tongue. "Wife."

"Hey." She felt him nuzzle the crown of her hair. "There's no blame here. It wasn't like I was a devoted penpal. Besides, there's no guarantee I would have gotten your messages. Not where we were."

"So where were—" His hold on her tightened, de-railing Becky's question. Deliberately? Had something changed between them? Or was he drifting again? Just what had Zachariah and his men been doing that he couldn't—or wouldn't—talk about it? The APO address and military domain name that he'd sent her several weeks after his departure had told her as little about his location and assignment as his brief messages had. Outside of the base headquarters where his unit had reported in between missions, he and his comrades seemed to have disappeared for weeks, even months, at a time. "Are you okay?"

Captain Somber here was so not playing into the let's-recapture-what-we-had-but-I-really-need-to-keep-it-light-so-I-can-walk-away-without-either-of-us-getting-hurt scenario she'd planned for this weekend. Was he normally this moody? She hadn't seen any indication of a darker side to Zachariah Clark back in D.C.

Beyond the military information he couldn't share, *taciturn* and *evasive* were hardly words she'd use to describe her conversations with Zachariah back then. Not that they'd had any deep heart-to-hearts. He'd been so refreshingly up front about what he wanted from her that Becky had found his lack of an agenda as much of an attraction as the breadth of those muscled shoulders and chest. He'd been blunt. He'd been bold. He'd worn his thoughts and emotions on his sleeve, and Becky had responded to his easy forthrightness.

The Zachariah Clark who'd gotten off the bus this morning was too complex for her to read, and that left her at an unfamiliar disadvantage. Becky couldn't be sure he would understand, much less welcome, the things she had to say and do—not if he was feeling down or preoccupied like this. And her concern about whatever was troubling him complicated her own promises to hurry back to the people who really needed her, people she could actually help.

This was supposed to be a welcome-home celebration. Escaping for a weekend frolic with her…um…husband.

Damn. Even *thinking* the word pinched at her conscience.

Oh, yeah. This reunion was going really well.

Zachariah gave her a quick bear hug before pulling away completely, beyond arm's reach, distancing himself from her questions as well as her touch. "I suppose if we'd had time to go through the newlywed training, we'd have done a better job of keeping in touch."

Becky arched one eyebrow. Did she know *anything* about Zachariah's life? "There's newlywed training?"

"Yeah. So the new spouse knows what to expect when the husband or wife is deployed. Where to find support groups. How to contact us if there's an emergency. Familiarizing each of us with what can be said in a message and what can't. Stuff like that." He lifted his cap, scratched his fingers over his ultra-short, fawn-colored hair and wedged the cap back on. "Sorry. I guess I cheated you out of all that by gettin' hitched so quick. I kind of ran off and left you in the dark." He turned his left hand back and forth, studying his splayed fingers as if seeing them in front of his face reminded him of something he didn't like. "Hell. I never even took the time to buy us rings."

Two small boys, darting around the fringe of a family welcoming home the father, accidentally bumped into the back of Zachariah's legs. He tensed instantly. His hand fisted and his shoulders seemed to expand in a way that made Becky think he was about to turn and attack. Only the Zachariah she knew didn't have a temper.

The boys must have sensed the brewing volcano, too.

"Sorry, mister," the little one chirped.

"He's a captain, dork-butt. Look at his collar."

"Sorry, Captain."

"Thanks for all you do for our country," the older one said, in a well-rehearsed voice.

"Yeah, thanks." The younger of the two boys stepped between Zachariah and Becky and craned his neck, squinching his mouth into a thoughtful frown as though he was perplexed by how far he had to look up to see Zachariah's face. "Do you know my dad?"

Zachariah blinked away whatever had seized him and looked over at the family gathering before lowering his chin and mustering half an apologetic grin for the boy. "Yeah. Sort of. He's in our support unit. We couldn't do our jobs without—"

"C'mon, Eric." The older boy put a hand on the young one's shoulder and pulled him away, apparently not trusting Zachariah's size or mood. "Dad's waiting for us. We get to carry his duffel bag."

As quickly as the boy's curiosity had surfaced, it disappeared. He chased his brother back to their family. "I get to carry it first!"

"Uh-uh!"

Zachariah scrubbed his palm down over his face and muttered a curse as he watched them disappear back into the crowd. "So how bad do you think I scared those kids?"

"Not half as much as you're scaring me." Becky propped her hands at the waist of her denim skirt. "You're acting like Zachariah Clark's evil twin. Are you going to tell me what's bugging you or not?"

His green eyes were the only thing that moved as his gaze bored into hers. "Like I said, I'm beat." *Leave it alone.* She understood the message clearly enough— didn't like it, but understood. An echo of silence passed before he shook loose his shoulders and twisted his neck from side to side, forcibly relaxing his posture if not convincing Becky he had truly relaxed.

"Then maybe we'd better get going," she suggested,

not knowing what more she could do, even if he were willing to share. She pointed toward the fence. "I'm parked in the visitors' lot. I can drive until we can get your truck out of storage."

With a nod, he heaved his duffel bag up onto his shoulder. After holding back for a moment, he lengthened his stride to fall into step beside her and settled his hand at the back of her waist. "Sorry. All the way home I was thinking about falling into bed. With you. I guess it was stupid to think nothing about us would change after eighteen months apart. This marriage thing takes a little getting used to."

"I know what you mean." It shamed her to think of how she'd kept the news of her *"gettin' hitched"* tucked away like a secret weapon in her back pocket—waiting until the moment was right to tell her parents, until now the secret weighed like an anchor around her neck. It was becoming more and more clear that there was more to making a marriage than a legal document. "It's as though we have to get reacquainted all over again."

And there was only one way they'd really known and understood each other, even back in D.C.

"I thought I was doing the right thing—making you my wife—in case something happened to me, or I got you pregnant. I just wanted you to know that what we had meant something to me."

Becky halted in her tracks. "I'm a big girl, Zachariah." She snagged his hand as he walked past. At that slightest of tugs, he stopped and looked down over his shoulder at her. "That week meant something to me, too. But you don't have to take care of me. You just have to…be with me. While you're here. While we're together." Her own plans, which she'd stewed over for months, were changing even as she spoke. "We'll figure out whatever we've missed in each other's lives later. For now, let's just try to stay in the moment, shall we?"

He considered the bargain, then altered his grip to lace his fingers together with hers and pull her to his side. "In the moment. Sure. I can do that. Now take me to your car."

She pointed toward the gate. "Over there."

He shifted direction and guided them through the fringes of the lingering crowd. He dipped his head to her ear so she could hear him as they hurried past the band, which was playing a Sousa march. "In your last e-mail, you mentioned something about that honey-moon we missed?"

His lips stayed close and nuzzled the sensitive skin beneath her earlobe.

Honeymoon. She liked the sound of that. Becky wound her other hand around Zachariah's and hugged herself against his arm. The brush of his lips and heat off his skin sparked something prickly and needy inside her. Maybe this awkward tension between them was nothing more than frustrated physical energy. Maybe once they got the lust—which had been sim-mering for eighteen months—out of their systems, everything else would fall into place. They could talk. He could lighten up. She could walk away.

Becky stumbled over the momentary hesitation of her feet. *Don't go there.*

But, linked to the brace of Zachariah's arm, she

couldn't fall. And because it had to be brief, she didn't want to retreat from the time they could be spending together. Not wanting to shout, she waited until the band was behind them before she answered, "I might have an idea or two in mind about that honeymoon."

"Spread those ideas out. Other than a quick visit to my folks out in Nebraska, you've got me for six whole weeks."

Six weeks? Um, yeah. About that…

"Unless you want to come with me?" he offered. "The ranch should be green and pretty in the middle of summer—the lake water nice and cool."

Nebraska? Ranch? Lake water? "Do you go sailing?"

"It's not that big a lake. Fishing, mostly." He released her hand and slipped his arm around her waist, pulling her flush to his side and hurrying their pace. "But I was thinking more along the lines of skinny-dipping after midnight."

In lake water? "Is that sanitary?"

"Sanitary? Man, you sure know how to sweet-talk a guy. Here I am, imagining the moonlight on your bare skin, and you're worried about the greeblies in the water."

"So there *is* something in the water."

"Fish. Hence, the fishing." He grinned. "Where's your sense of adventure?"

She tensed. *In the moment. Stay in the moment.* "You told me you live on a ranch. Don't the cows use the water, too—"

"Yo, Clarksie!"

Becky jumped in her skin as a man materialized from between two parked cars and charged toward them, his arm outstretched. He was big, not by Zachariah standards, but big enough that everything inside Becky jerked with the urge to run in the opposite direction.

Zachariah braced for an instant in a protective stance between her and the man. Then the tension rolled off his shoulders along with his duffel bag and he released her to stick out his own hand to greet the man with a handshake. "Action Man!"

While Becky squashed down the startled heartbeat that pounded in her chest, she took note of the dark royal pants and khaki shirt that marked "Action Man" as another military officer. The handshake became a bear hug that involved backslapping, ribald nicknames and seeing who could squeeze the other harder.

Clearly an old friend, judging by the rapid-fire questions about families and work and the "How've you beens?"

Not a threat.

Not even anything to do with her.

Way to play it cool, Owens.

The dressed-up Marine pulled an athletic-looking woman up beside him and tucked her under his arm. "I'm as good-lookin' as ever and I've got some of the best prospects I've had in a long time. This is Tess."

"Tess, eh? I'm Zachariah Clark."

The woman named Tess smiled and took his hand. "I've heard a lot about you, Clarksie. Most of it, I couldn't repeat to my mother. But to hear Trav tell it, it's all good. Welcome home."

"Aw, shucks. Thanks, ma'am." Zachariah leaned forward. "Is she the one you e-mailed me about?"

The man named Travis didn't even hesitate. "She's the one, period. I've still got some details to work out, but—"

As embarrassed by her knee-jerk reaction as she was relieved, Becky took a deep breath and stepped forward to be introduced. "Do I have to hang back like the paparazzi? Or do I get an introduction, too?"

"Geez. Sorry, darlin'." Quickly shifting his stance to pull Becky into the conversation, Zachariah rested his hand at the small of her back and made the introductions. "Travis McCormick, this is my…my wife." The fingers at her back contracted. An apology? Or did the word feel as awkward on his tongue as it had on hers? "This is Becky Owens. Becky *Clark*." The fingers tightened another notch and she felt his gaze sweep across her face. "This is the Beckster."

Like their missing wedding rings, her new name was another topic they'd never had a chance to discuss.

A cheesy grin split Travis's face. "What, you forget you were married already?"

They moved past the awkward moment with more handshakes and an introduction to Travis's girl-friend, Tess Bartlett, whom Becky learned was a physical therapist.

"So how do you know Zachariah, Captain McCormick?" Becky asked, curious to meet one of his friends.

"It's Travis, and don't worry about the title." Despite the woman at his side, Travis seemed to be a bit of a flirt. "Clarksie and I served together on a Special Operations team—until I got wounded."

At the mention of the word *wounded,* the good-natured camaraderie between the two men ebbed as though they were rowdy boys who'd been repri-manded by their parents for too much roughhousing. Becky could sense the stiffness that crept into Zachariah's posture.

"I see you're not in Charlie uniform—your camou-flage work gear," Zachariah pointed out. "Does that mean the top brass denied your request to return to a Special Ops team?"

Travis waved aside his concern. "I didn't give them the chance. I asked to be transferred to the training division. General Craddock approved it yesterday. I'm going to be teaching the yahoos who'll be taking your place one day."

"Congratulations, man." Becky glanced up. Despite a smile, Zachariah's jaw had tensed. "What changed your mind?"

"I realized I couldn't give the hundred-and-ten percent S.O. teams need anymore. But I figure I can eke out about a hundred-and-one percent to whip some of those new boys into shape. I've learned I make a pretty good coach."

Seeing the blush that dotted Tess's cheeks when Travis smiled down at her, Becky had to wonder just what kind of "coaching" Zachariah's pal was talking about.

"I get to choose my own staff." Travis jabbed Zacha-riah on the shoulder and grinned. "I could use a big hard-ass like you on the team."

Zachariah's hand fisted at Becky's back before he broke contact completely. "I'll think about it."

"Do. I can always use a man with good hands."

Afraid she was witnessing another reappearance of the secretive stranger who'd been so intense that he'd frightened two little boys, Becky linked her arm through Zachariah's. "Can't we all?"

Tess and Travis laughed right along with her, the double entendre buying a few seconds, giving Zachariah's mood a chance to pass. His deep, rumbly laugh finally joined in. He linked his fingers together with Becky's and lifted her hand to claim it with a kiss.

Like the laugh, she couldn't tell if his silent thankyou was for real or for show. Still, his words sounded sincere enough. "Duty calls. Thanks for showing up, Trav. It feels good to be on home soil. Good to see you."

Travis nodded. "Well, you've got a homecoming I'm not going to keep you from any longer. Take care, buddy."

"You, too." The two men shook hands. "I'll call you soon, I promise."

Travis looked at Becky, then up at Zachariah and winked. "I'd give it a good forty-eight hours or so before you make any phone calls. I expect you're gonna be busy for a while."

THE MAN OPENED HIS TOP RIGHT desk drawer and pulled out papers and file folders until he uncovered the photograph at the bottom.

After a quick glance around his bustling office to verify that he was alone and unwatched, he pulled on a pair of plastic gloves and reached in to touch the picture. Clarified and enlarged on his home computer, the photo provided a remarkable likeness of the woman captured there. He traced his fingertip around the woman's wide, slightly crooked mouth, lingering on the natural pout that was evident even on this unsmiling government ID.

He liked that mouth better when it was closed.

She was pretty enough, in a Rubenesque kind of way. Her hair was so blond, it nearly hurt the eyes to look at it straight on in full sunlight. And the expensive layered cut she wore it in spoke of family money rather than a government salary.

She was class.

She was style.

"You bitch."

A familiar rage sparked through his blood.

"You think you're going to make the world fall into place the way you want it, don't you?" He splayed his fingers over her face and squeezed his eyes shut, breathing deeply to control the anger. Breathing deeper to control the animalistic urges that fired through his body. "I gave you every chance to do right by me. To understand the way things should be. But you just like to screw with a man when he's down, don't you? Makes you feel like you're something special, doesn't it? Like you're too high and mighty to ever fall off your throne."

Still smothering her face with his palm, he opened another drawer and pulled out the envelope he'd brought from home. "I'm going to put you in your place, Princess. If you're going to deny me what should be mine, then I'm going to destroy you. I'm going to make you suffer. I want to see you weeping. And if you still don't learn your lesson…

"I'm going to kill you."

3

ZACHARIAH KNEW HIS MAMA WOULD have had his hide if she'd been there to see him in action that morning.

As he followed the enticing bounce of Becky's bottom to her car, he had only one thing on his mind. And it wasn't the apology he needed to make.

He'd like to think he had a fever—or blame it on eighteen months of celibacy or on the memorial service he'd attended two days ago at the base. But something wasn't right in his head. From the moment he'd spotted Becky's deep blue eyes, he'd been drawn to her like a moth to a back porch light. If he could just get to her, get a hold of her—get inside her—then everything would feel right again.

The crap that had been plaguing him since that last mission into Al-Bazan would fade away. He could replay the awful way he'd reacted to those two kids—acting like the enemy instead of a colleague to their daddy. Maybe he could get a laugh out of them instead of instilling in them the urge to run away. He'd be able to stand back for a moment and figure out why he'd snapped at Becky for calling him on his behavior, and why he'd held something back from his best friend, Travis McCormick.

He was happy to be stateside. Happy to see Travis back on the job and looking as fit and fine as ever. Happy to find his woman—his new wife—waiting for him now that he was officially off duty.

But from the moment Becky had launched herself into his arms and her sweet, full lips had softened beneath his, Zachariah had been waging a war inside himself. Fighting to control a battle between a shameless hard-on and the seething emotions that itched at him like intel of an ambush. He knew all hell was gonna break loose—he just didn't know when or where it would happen. And he wasn't sure he could control the situation.

He hadn't controlled a damn thing in Al-Bazan.

Shit. Zachariah crushed the strap of his duffel bag in his fist and slammed the door on the memories that tried to escape. He blinked himself out of that desert hellhole with the dead bodies and acrid smoke, and concentrated every bit of his considerable will on counting the number of metal buttons running down the side of Becky's blue-jean skirt. He hoped to hell that thing had a zipper on it.

He desperately needed to recapture the normalcy of his life here in the States. And *normal* with Becky meant something blessedly physical. The lacy V-neck blouse she wore, which covered up enough to look classy and ladylike while still clinging in all the right spots to remind him of the size and weight and beauty of her breasts, didn't help. Neither did the deep rose of her painted toenails or the alabaster skin showing beneath the hem of her skirt.

He was horny. He was simmering. He was full of a need that went beyond basic sex and had him ready to bust out of his skin.

Yet he had to make nice. He had to be civilized. After all, he was stateside. He was off duty. He was home.

But Zachariah didn't want to reminisce or discuss new job opportunities or listen to small talk.

He wanted Becky.

Now.

If he could just recapture the mindless perfection of that week they'd spent together in D.C., he could get this fever out of his system. He could feel like himself again. He could cope.

"This is it. Shall we?" With a sweeping flair as stylish as any game-show model's, Becky pointed to a silver, late-model Nissan sedan. She pulled a ring of keys from her pocket. "You can put your bag in the back."

She opened the trunk and Zachariah dropped his duffel inside, inhaling a whiff of her warm, exotic perfume as he bent beside her. The remembered scent filled his head and his fantasies, and he scooped her up into his arms as he turned back around.

"I missed you, darlin'." He'd kissed off all her lipstick earlier, but her nude pink lips seemed to beckon him all the more. "I can't wait until we're alone together."

Her mouth was soft and hot and eager beneath the claim of his lips. Becky wound her arms around his neck and pulled herself into his kiss. Her lips parted. Her tongue danced against his. Breasts pillowed against the ache in his chest, her nipples beaded, branding him.

Humming her needy sound, which was as potent as a caress, she hooked her tongue around his and pulled it into her mouth. *Aw, geez.* Zachariah's body lurched in response, mimicking the same push-pull gesture. With one arm still anchored around her waist, he slid his hand down over the curve of her butt and boosted her up, aligning their bodies together like snug puzzle pieces. Her skirt inched higher as he found naked skin and dragged his palm over the back of her velvety thigh.

Zachariah's blood was humming right along with her seductive moans. This was the way it had been between them in D.C. The way it should be between them. Just them. Just this.

But with a breathless laugh, Becky pulled her fingers from his hair and slipped them between their lips. "We're not exactly alone yet. People are watching."

"They're jealous." Though a weak voice inside his head backed her up with the message that this was neither the time nor the place to relieve their sexual frustration, his body wasn't listening. He kissed her fingertips, working his way back to her mouth. "Tell 'em to get their own girl. You're taken."

With a laugh that jiggled against his chest, she pushed his chin up into the air. "Not yet, I'm not. But I trust you'll see to that later?"

She was killin' him with her lush body and naughty double entendres. But he discovered he still knew how to laugh as he lowered her back to the ground, testing that suddenly shaky will of his by enduring the friction of her soft curves along his harder planes. Once she was standing on her own again, he adjusted her skirt to a more modest level and tried to breathe some sanity back into his brain. He touched his forehead to hers, grinning at the stain of passion he'd stamped onto her swollen lips. "Have I told you how happy I am to see you?"

The blue-eyed temptress palmed the hardest part of him through his pants. "I *know* how happy you are to see me, big guy."

Zachariah jerked in her grip, squeezed his eyes shut and silently begged for strength.

"Beckster…" he warned. Audience or not, if she didn't move her hand, he was going to finish what they'd started. Here. Now.

Becky released him and stepped back, holding her hands out to either side as if she were surrendering to his plea. But that clever, daring look in her eyes told him she was taking charge rather than giving in. "Get in. You can nap while I drive since I can't guarantee how much sleep you'll be getting once we reach our destination."

"A woman after my own heart." He leaned down to kiss her again, but Becky was made of stronger stuff and his lips skidded over her cheek as she dodged his mouth and nudged him toward the side of the car.

"Get in."

"Yes, ma'am." After closing the trunk, Zachariah climbed down into the passenger seat. Even sliding the seat all the way back, he had to fold himself in like a pretzel and lean against the door to keep his shoulder from bumping into hers. He barely had room to spread his legs far enough apart to give his woody a chance to relax. He removed his cap, but still had little clearance between his crewcut and the roof. "Oh, man. Why don't you just put me in a sardine can?"

He hadn't known how small a sporty little Nissan could be. Definitely no room for playing in here. The cramped space should be incentive enough for him to be a good boy and mind his manners a little while longer.

"I won't ask if you're comfy," she apologized, backing out and pulling into traffic. "But I do promise it'll be a short drive."

Short was a relative term that had more to do with time than distance. The way Becky Owens—make that Becky *Clark,* he amended—put the pedal to the metal, she should be driving at Daytona instead of zipping along the highway that connected the Marine base in Quantico to the outskirts of Washington, D.C.

"We're not heading down to Richmond?" He knew she lived in Virginia's state capital. With his base housing surrendered and his stuff all in storage, he'd just assumed they'd be spending the next several hours at her place.

She shook her head as she checked her mirror and zipped between a semi and a pickup truck. Zachariah gripped the dashboard and held on. Forget Daytona. This woman could be driving on the battlefield, dodging incoming fire. How had he missed her lead foot tendencies before? Had they really not gone anywhere besides hotel rooms and the courthouse?

"So was your flight home really that bad?"

He grinned as they sped past a string of cars and cut over to catch the exit ramp. "It lasted about twenty-seven hours longer than this trip is gonna take."

Becky downshifted and adjusted her speed to merge with the city traffic. "And you don't have to be anywhere for a while?"

This polite chitchat wasn't on his to-do list.

"As of ten-hundred hours this morning, I'm on leave to do whatever the hell I want for forty-two days. And you know what I want to do." He reached over and traced a finger along the line of her jaw before winding it into her pale golden hair. The chin-length silk tumbled over the back of his hand like a thousand tiny kisses. She'd cut her hair since he'd seen her last, but one thing sure hadn't changed. She was still icy cool to look at, but fiery to the touch. His touch, at any rate.

Her full lips pouted with a smile as she turned to kiss that finger before batting him away to keep her focus on the road. "I want that, too. I rented a room at that same hotel we stayed at after that first night at Groucho's Pub."

Yeah. The night they'd first met. The night they'd first had sex. The night Zachariah had first started to wonder if the bachelor's life was all it was cracked up to be. Not when he could come home every night to something as smart, sassy and sexy as Becky Owens.

Becky *Clark*. He winced at the name that refused to click into place inside his head. Maybe if she'd say it. Just once.

But talking was for later. Though he'd showered and gotten some shut-eye before boarding the bus to the base, Zachariah was beat. Eighteen months on active duty, running more missions than he could count—he swallowed hard and pushed his thoughts right on past that last mission that had gone so wrong so fast—and an endless flight did that to a man. No matter what kind of fighting shape he was in.

"Stay in the moment," Becky had said. Sounded like good advice. No past. No future. Just now. Just them. He leaned back against the headrest and let his eyes drift shut.

She'd warned him he needed to take a nap before she got him back to the hotel. He intended to do her bidding in whatever she asked of him.

But the name issue wouldn't seem to let him be. Maybe it was his fault as much as hers that it was an awkward point of discomfort between them. "Hey, sorry about that whole confusion with the 'wife' thing when I was introducing you to Travis. I guess when he startled us, I kind of lost my train of thought."

"No problem. It's not something we need to concern ourselves with right now. I'm content to go with plain old Becky Owens. Don't worry about it."

Zachariah winked one eye open. No problem? Was her response to his apology just a little too glib to be sincere? Or was his weary brain reading something into the fierce grip she had on her steering wheel? "You sure? I mean, it wasn't an intentional stumble. Becky Clark. Becky Owens-Clark. However you want to say it, I'm proud to claim you as mine."

"I know." Did her knuckles just turn a little whiter around the steering wheel?

Zachariah shook his head and let his eye close once more. Too much thinking. He needed sleep. He needed sex. He needed Becky. "I'm not used to saying it out loud. One minute we're in front of a justice of the peace, and the next I'm on my way to Reagan International to catch my plane to...hell."

Even if he was cleared to talk about Al-Bazan now, he didn't want to say the words out loud. The memories were like poison stirring in the pit of his stomach. And he was pretty sure it was the past few months trying to sneak into his thoughts—not Becky's speedway driving—that was making him a tad queasy.

She shifted the car and slowed for a turn. Then he jumped when she reached farther across the front seat and squeezed his thigh. "Don't sweat it. We're going to stay in the here and now, remember? Let's enjoy the homecoming before we worry about anything else."

Zachariah's eyes popped open. There *was* something to worry about.

But before he could ask what it might be, her hand slid higher. Closer to the action. The electric current that had been buzzing through his body ever since that kiss in the parking lot zinged up to a higher voltage. Just like that. He was hard. He was ready.

"Beckster." His warning was a low-pitched growl in his throat. "I can't maneuver in this car."

She dutifully returned both hands to the wheel. "Then you'd better lean back and relax. Like I said, you're going to need your strength."

With that husky promise lacing her voice, Zachariah could have damn well found a way to maneuver.

But he was smart enough to know when to advance and when to retreat. It would be a good idea if they actually got to the hotel in one piece—and without having to explain themselves to a traffic cop if they got pulled over for reckless, er…driving.

He could forget. For now.

He could wait. A little.

Closing his eyes, Zachariah leaned back against the headrest. But even with the deep breathing exercise that normally relaxed him, sleep wasn't coming. With every inhale, his nose filled with the spice of Becky's perfume. With every exhale, his mind filled with images of each delicious thing he was going to do with her once they reached their destination.

"Becky?"

"Yes?"

"Drive faster."

BECKY PULLED INTO THE Wardman Park Hotel's circular drive. It was sentimentality as much as the desire to put distance between her and the problems waiting for her back in Richmond that had prompted her to make this reservation. But a momentary glitch in her courage tried to surface as she thought back to the last time she'd been here with Captain Zachariah Clark.

Checking into the posh, discreet hotel with a man she'd just met in a bar—okay, after getting better acquainted with his hands and mouth in the parking lot outside the bar—had to be the craziest thing she'd ever done.

Correction. The second craziest.

She'd avoided dealing with number one on her crazy list longer than she'd allow any of her clients to put off such an important decision. But she didn't intend to ruin tonight's festivities by addressing the marriage issue now.

Squelching the nagging misgivings over the conversation she knew they needed to have, Becky parked the car. *Stay in the moment.* That would be her treat for herself this weekend.

No past. No future.

No family.

No clients.

No messages for the *bitch* who was ruining her anonymous fan's life.

Becky shivered in the summer heat as the tension filled her, then gradually dissipated with a mental affirmation of her resolve.

She was going to do this. She *wanted* to do this. With Zachariah Clark she could enjoy the here and now. She could let out the sensual, decadent side of her that had no place in the rest of her life. She had a man to welcome home after serving overseas in a war zone. And from the look—and feel—of things, the big guy needed some serious welcoming.

Becky looked over at him dozing in the tiny confines of her car and smiled. She was torn between the soft tug at her heart at his deep, soft snore—indicating just how exhausted he must be after being on guard every waking moment for the past eighteen months—and the firmer tug at her libido. Zachariah was an adrenaline rush to her hormones. There was just so much of him. So much muscle. Such broad shoulders and long legs—like tree trunks. Such big hands with an amazing coordination that must reflect in his work as well as his loving. And the whole of him was in fine, fighting shape. So much man. So much to want.

Tiny muscles, deep in her belly, clenched and yearned just looking at him. She licked her lips, feeling a sudden thirst as she ran her gaze over his wide, firm mouth. His square jaw. The bump on his nose—a remnant from an old fight, perhaps? One he'd no doubt won. She visually caressed the strong brow and masculine crop of sandy-brown hair that framed his commanding, if not handsome, face.

Becky slowly exhaled, letting the warm breeze of her desire dance across his skin.

One bold green eye opened and met her gaze. "I told you I can't maneuver in here, darlin'."

Oh, yeah. Conversations could definitely wait. She wanted this. She stretched up and pressed her lips to his cheek in a mild hint of things to come. "Then get out. We're here."

Suddenly, it was a race to get checked in and carry their bags up to the room. They scrambled to hang the Do Not Disturb sign on the knob and then locked the door behind them.

And then Zachariah had her backed against the door. The buttons of her blouse flew by the wayside. His hands were on her breasts, lifting, squeezing, flicking the nipples to attention through the silk of her bra. She gasped as the instant fire rocketed from the tips of her breasts down to the juncture of her thighs. No man had touched her like this. Ever.

Ever. She groaned aloud as he dipped his head and

guided one straining peak to his mouth, swirling his tongue around the distended tip. "Oh-h."

Becky needed something to hold on to as her knees went weak. She needed him.

Winding her arms around Zachariah's neck, she skimmed her palms against the prickly grain of his hair, slipping her fingers up beneath his hat and tossing it aside so she could cup his head and drag his mouth up to hers.

She paused only long enough to meet the hungry desire blazing in his verdant eyes, long enough for him to see that same hunger reflected in her own. "I'm glad you're safe. I'm glad you're with me. Welcome home."

Then their lips met. His, hard and demanding. Hers, soft but eager to make some demands of their own. He took. She gave. She begged. He delivered.

She got his shirt off him, his belt undone. Her skirt and half-slip were on the floor. She grasped at the hem of his T-shirt and he reached for her panties.

"Do you have protection handy?" he rasped against her ear before nipping at the lobe. "Mine are in the bottom of my duffel."

Becky nodded, pushing the T-shirt up over ridges of muscle and a scar that hadn't been there eighteen months ago. Touching the puckered skin at the flat of his stomach, she glimpsed a similar scar cutting through the eagle's wing tattooed on his bicep. "What are these?"

He tongued the side of her neck, ignoring her concern. "We need condoms. Quick."

Right. Stay in the moment. Ask questions later.

"Okay."

Weak with desire, Becky stumbled to the desk, where her overnight bag had landed. The shock of losing his heat and his determined touch left her breathing uneven, her fingers uncoordinated. By the time she'd unzipped her bag, spilled the box of condoms, cursed and fished out one of the shiny silver wrappers, Zachariah was naked and looming in the mirror behind her.

Oh, my.

Taller than she remembered. Bigger. Harder.

Her body wet with an instant female response to the potently male sight.

"I'm hurrying," she whispered, her throat not working any better than her clumsy fingers.

"Now, darlin'." His arousal nudged against her bottom as he easily reached over her shoulder and plucked the wrapper from her hands.

Fine. While he ripped and rolled, she could use the extra minute to take off her blouse and unhook her bra.

But Zachariah didn't give her an extra minute.

He poked her again as he closed in behind her. He looped his right forearm around her waist to absorb the blunt of the desk's hard edge as he pushed her up against it. "I need this." His left hand slipped between her thighs and parted her. "I'll make it good for you the next time, I promise."

Becky automatically braced her hands on the polished mahogany surface as his chest met her back and they leaned forward together. "It's okay. I'm read—"

He entered her in one deep, sharp thrust. Becky

gasped as the tip of his cock nudged at her G-spot. "Ah-h…" She couldn't speak as tendrils of pain melted into the prelude to pleasure.

He held himself still inside her for several endless seconds, filling her, stretching her as her body adjusted to accommodate him. She felt the vibration of every muscle he held in check, from the open mouth wetting the nape of her neck to the engorged member buried inside her.

"I'm sorry," he panted against her skin. "Next… time…promise…"

Zachariah quickly withdrew. He widened his stance, adjusting his hips to cup her bottom. One hand slid to her breast, the other down toward her clit. She looked up into the mirror and found his green gaze locked onto hers.

Becky nodded.

With only one sleeve off and a bra strap riding down her arm, Becky fancied herself a wanton woman as Zachariah plunged inside her a second time. He ground his hips into her bottom, lifting her toes off the carpet as he bent her forward and rammed himself in to the hilt, roaring with his release. As he pinched her nipple, rubbed hard at her swollen nub, she writhed helplessly, suspended between his body and the desk, trapped between his hands and cock.

On a short fuse of desire herself, the pressure building inside her detonated.

Becky cried out. Her arms went weak.

Good? It didn't get any better than this raw, over-whelming need.

Next time? *Oh God, yes.*

And when she collapsed against the desk in the sheer exhaustion at being so desired, so taken, so satiated, Zachariah picked her up and carried her to bed.

4

"…VIOLATED THE RESTRAINING order, then call…slap his butt in jail." The distant voice spoke threatening gibberish and disjointed phrases in Zachariah's dream. "I don't care what Sligh told you. I represent you now. He'll pay it, Dimitra. That's what *I'm* here for."

Zachariah rolled over onto his side and nestled his rough cheek down into a pillow of softness with a smile. *Yeah.* He hadn't generated a fantasy like this one for a while. It was a woman's voice in his dream. A sexy woman, judging by the blend of confidence and huskiness in her tone—some tough chick who wasn't taking any guff off anyone. He liked a woman who could stand up to trouble. That meant she could stand up to him.

"Call the cops. Yes, I know. But that's my problem, not yours…check on you as soon as I'm back in Richmond. Sometime this…call them. Or I will."

The woman went away for a while, but when the hushed tones returned, he realized it was Becky's voice. Zachariah grinned as he dozed. Definitely a sexy woman. Unexpectedly beautiful in ways that made his hormones crazy. "Dad? Yes, it's me again. Now tell me exactly what…"

Becky was a tough chick. Oh, she might class up the exterior with tailored clothes and ten-dollar words, but there was nothing but steel running through her graceful backbone.

Zachariah pushed aside the covers and flipped onto his back, keeping his ear attuned to the fading voice, hoping she'd issue a command to him like she had before they'd fallen asleep. *"Touch me here. Kiss me. I need you in me. Now!"* Or maybe he was cooling off his body, which automatically heated up as fantasies turned into memories of Becky and the afternoon and night they'd shared.

Yeah, that first time, he'd shown all the finesse of a rutting bull. It had been a catharsis for him—a blinding expression of long-denied hunger and a driving need to find acceptance and humanity and healing. The second time had been a little more civilized. It had involved the bed and some champagne and using each other as wineglasses before rolling her onto her back and burying himself inside her. By the time he'd carried her out of the shower and they'd done it for a third time, Zachariah had been well and truly exhausted. Time zone changes and sleepless nights and mind-numbing sex had all caught up with him and he'd crashed. The bed was clean and comfy; Becky was warm by his side. His physical needs were sated enough for the time being that he could fall into a deep, long slumber.

Maybe that heavy, restorative sleep was what made him so groggy now as he tried to rouse himself enough to understand Becky's urgent whispers. She must be on her cell phone, pacing, judging by the ebb and flow of volume. Talking softly, but not talking to him—unless his sleep-addled brain was translating her words into things that didn't make sense. "Is she okay?"

Was *who* okay? The king-size mattress shifted as she sank down onto the opposite edge. Becky was all right, wasn't she? Even though he'd been rougher than he'd intended that first time, she hadn't complained last night.

In fact, the only one he knew definitely wasn't okay was Lance Corporal Watson. And a half-dozen rebel insurgents with murder on their minds.

Watson.

Shit.

Dreams of a busty blonde in his bed vanished in a poof of harsh reality as the familiar nightmare crept out of a dark corner of his mind and seized control of his thoughts. Zachariah twisted on the bed, but he wasn't conscious enough to scare it away.

"Where the hell…? Watson! Fall back! Fall back!"

"I can reach it, sir!"

"Negative! We regroup now!"

"Just one more second."

"Get your ass out of there, Marine! It's gonna blow!"

"I almost—"

"Watson!"

All at once, Zachariah was gritty and greasy, slick with sweat. His nostrils burned from the fiery heat raining down around him. His gut and shoulder burned even hotter. The rebels were neutralized, civilian casualties, zero. A successful mission by top-brass standards.

Gutsy kid. A real Marine. A real hero.

Stunned from his own wounds, Zachariah dragged his feet, carrying what was left of Darrell Watson's body back to the checkpoint.

It should have been him. Not this green kid with the stupid jokes and a picture of his mom in his pocket. It was *his* bomb to disarm, damn it! *His* responsibility! Watson shouldn't have taken the risk. If only the kid would have waited five seconds as he'd ordered. Five seconds! He shouldn't have been there. Zachariah should have wrestled the corporal's skinny butt to the ground and blown the charge himself before the timer ticked down on them. Watson shouldn't be dead. Zachariah should have kept the kid safe.

Ah, hell. He couldn't get away from the fire and the guilt. He couldn't escape. *Ah, hell.*

"Zachariah?"

A distant voice blipped through his imagination as Zachariah fought with the haunting shadows. Sequestered together like this, nothing should be able to get to him or Becky. Al-Bazan was thousands of miles away, yet it had somehow invaded this very room.

Darrell Watson was dead. He should have kept him safe.

But all he'd been able to do was stand guard over a closed casket and watch Darrell's mother cry.

"Zachariah. Can you hear me?"

He felt a warm touch at his face, another pressed against his heart.

"Zachariah. Wake up."

Clinging to the lifeline of that commanding voice,

Zachariah struggled to obey. His subconscious mind sorted reality from nightmare, and he woke with a start.

With every muscle locked on guard against the terrors of that night, Zachariah opened his eyes to find Becky's face hovering above him. Her rich, cobalt eyes were lined with concern. She'd climbed onto the middle of the bed to shake him out of that dark place where he'd gone.

"Are you okay?" Those unblinking eyes were daring him to deny the truth.

Zachariah sat up straight and sucked in a deep breath that nudged his shoulder against her. She quickly jerked away as if the contact had singed her. What the hell?

He must have said something in his sleep, done something that alarmed her—hell, he could have scared the crap out of her for all he knew.

"I was having a bad dream," he admitted, keeping any details about post-traumatic stress to himself. He kept silent about his survivor's guilt, and his overdeveloped sense of responsibility, which the unit psychologist had discussed with him at his hospital discharge meeting. *Hell.* He only had a few weeks of leave to share with Becky. He didn't intend to spoil any of his time with her by hashing out the emotional baggage lurking inside him. These few weeks were the break he needed to get his head back in the game. Becky was what he needed.

"It's more than that," she insisted.

He knew it. She knew it. But he'd be damned if he was going to waste one minute of their honeymoon talking through his problems. He could go back to base and make an appointment with the psychologist for that. He had other things he preferred to do with his wife.

Zachariah reached out to sift her silky hair between his fingers. "I'm sorry, darlin'. I didn't mean to…" That's when he focused in on the tiny, hands-free cell phone hooked around her ear. Leaning over him, her hair had masked it. But now he saw not only the phone, but also the black cord linked to the receiver in her hand, and the button she was pushing to mute their exchange from whoever was on the line with her. Pulling back, he nodded toward the earpiece. "Finish your call."

She eyed him a few seconds longer, and Zachariah had to look away before she scooted off the edge of the bed and pushed the button again. "You still there? No, I had something I needed to take care of." She walked away, pacing the length of the room as she resumed her conversation. "I said I was fine, didn't I? Now tell me about the call."

Zachariah hated the idea that Becky thought she needed to take care of him. It wasn't so much a matter of wounded pride as it was one of practicality. He needed to get past Watson's death and the guilt he felt without dumping on her. He needed to handle the nightmares himself. The men in his unit were *his* responsibility. *He* was in charge of not only getting the job done, but of keeping everyone safe. He was in command for a reason—because he could deal with the pressure, the snap judgments in the heat of battle. He could cope with whatever happened in whatever way it went down.

As the officer in charge of his Spec Ops unit, with a specialty in explosives and demolition, he wasn't supposed to need anybody's help. He wasn't supposed to fail.

Despite his turbulent thoughts, the bright sunlight filtering through the sheer curtains at the window warmed his face and chest and seeped into the dark corners of his brain. Al-Bazan was miles away, weeks behind him. Zachariah released the crumpled sheets from his fists and arranged the covers over his bare lap. He forced himself to breathe deeply, evenly, and let his gaze drift over his surroundings, orienting himself to the luxurious, antique comfort of the hotel room.

Soft, creamy cotton and air conditioning brushed his skin. The clean scents of soap and Becky's familiar exotic spice teased his nose. He was in Washington, D.C. Back in civilization. In a swanky haven of a hotel room.

With Becky.

"…one-sided dialogue here. No. All right. Fine, I'll try my best. But I have a life."

Fully awake and in control of himself once more, Zachariah turned his attention to something much more pleasant than his nightmares. His…*wife.*

He smiled. It sounded more and more right each time he said or thought the word.

He watched her turn and pace back toward the bed. When he made eye contact, she winked. But her attention was still tuned to the conversation in her ear. She shook her head. "I have a schedule to keep. Responsibilities."

"Sounds serious." Zachariah tossed the sheet aside

and scooted to the foot of the bed. He snagged her hand as she neared and gave a little tug to pull her into his lap.

But she braced a hand on his shoulder and mouthed the word *please* before squeezing his fingers, offering an apologetic sigh and pushing away. She hurried to the far side of the room, still listening to whoever was on the line with her.

Denied a cuddle and the chance to prove he was one hundred percent fit for fighting—or loving—Zachariah breathed a wistful sigh of his own. He scrubbed his fingers over the itchy shadow of his beard and debated his next move. The bedside clock read 12:32. He was buck naked and Becky was fully dressed—in a black patterned skirt and ice-blue top that draped softly over her curves.

When the hell had she gotten up and done the whole shower/hair/makeup/gettin' gorgeous thing? How long had she been on the phone?

He tried to distance himself from the suspicion that his new wife had been up early and working for hours already, on this, the first morning of their honeymoon. Watching her in action eased some of the sting out of that notion. Despite her ladylike facade, Becky truly was that tough chick from his dreams. With his background, no wonder he got such a kick out of her telling him what was what, where to put it and when she wanted it.

She was all sharp-eyed and in control, and every step she took was as succinct as the articulation of her words. The only thing better than listening to that voice issue an order was watching that skirt swish against her firm, pale calves. And the only thing better than watching would be taking that skirt off and gettin' busy again. All of a sudden, Zachariah was feeling a whole new world of rested and ready for action. But he was also getting the distinct impression that Becky was done feeling frisky. Maybe he'd tuckered her out last night, too. Or maybe these phone calls were what had her out of the mood so soon.

"No, of course, I don't want that." She angled her back to him and lowered her voice. "Did *she* talk to him?" Her shoulders sagged with a long sigh. "Well, that's something, at least. But it never should have happened. Yes, it's my fault. I'm sorry. I'll take care of it. I'll *take care* of it," she repeated.

Whisper or not, Zachariah's ears worked just fine and he detected a different sort of tension in her voice. Not so articulate. Not so easy on the ears. Not so tough.

Zachariah's concern clicked up a notch. Just on alert. There was nothing he could put a finger on, only a sense that something wasn't right in Becky's world. Something besides him. He thought back to that uncharacteristic flinch of fear when his pal Travis had snuck up on them yesterday. Zachariah had blamed the impression on his own hyperawareness of the world around him.

He'd quickly recovered. It was Travis McCormick, after all, his best friend—a man he'd known since basic training. A man he'd trust his life with. Nothing to fear.

Yet Becky had also been afraid.

He watched her now as she tunneled her fingers beneath the fringe of hair at her nape and massaged the back of her neck. Did something still have her spooked?

Nah. Just his imagination. Becky Owens—*damn*—
Becky *Clark* was strong in ways that had nothing to
do with being physical. She'd been startled, not afraid.
This was fatigue. Stress, maybe. But not fear. He was
overthinking this. Just because he'd screwed up in Al-
Bazan didn't mean there was anything to worry about
here. There weren't demons waiting around every
corner. He wasn't at war anymore.

He was just out of sorts because the outside world
had intruded on their honeymoon. Last night had
taken the edge off his fierce need to connect with his
new wife—to feel human again. Now that he'd
gotten the worst of it out of his system, he could
afford to be a little patient. If she wasn't up for
mixing business with smooching right now, then
he'd hop into the shower and wake himself up good
and proper.

Five minutes later, the shower was beating clean and
healthy heat into his skin while shaving cream softened
his beard. But he paused after the first stroke of his
razor. Wait a minute. Mixing *business* with smooching? What happened to staying in the moment? Was
the honeymoon already over?

Zachariah quickly finished shaving and rinsed off.
After a few quick flicks of his towel, he wrapped the
white terry cloth low around his hips and walked out.
He and Becky had reversed positions from that last
morning they'd spent together in D.C. Only this time,
Zachariah had a sinking feeling that today wasn't
going to turn out to be anywhere near as much fun as
doing her right on this very vanity counter had been.

If he had more of an ego, he might be ticked to find his newlywed wife on the phone again.

"Clear as much as you can, Cheryl. These need to be my top priorities. Of course, you can wait until morning. Enjoy your date. But remember, first thing tomorrow. Thanks." Becky disconnected the call. But now she had a laptop computer out on the desk and was scrolling through pages on the screen.

Keep it cool, Clarksie.

"Trouble at work?" he asked.

Her shoulders stiffened for an instant before she spun around in the chair. Her gaze darted first to his shrapnel scars, then up to his face. A frown dimpled the middle of her forehead. *Oh, hell, no.* He was witnessing something he'd never expected to see on Becky's face. A lie forming. Or at least a half truth. "Yes. I'm sorry. That was my executive assistant on the phone. I asked for forty-eight hours off. Told my office that I wanted to remain incommunicado for the entire weekend. But something came up that can't wait until tomorrow. It's a mess."

Forty-eight hours? "You only asked for the weekend off for our honeymoon?"

What happened to his six weeks to rest and recover and get to know his new wife in every way possible?

Becky rose to her feet and slowly closed the distance between them. "I wanted to tell you when I picked you up at Quantico. But you weren't exactly in the mood to talk, and it seemed like the news would make things worse. I didn't want to do anything to spoil your homecoming." She stopped, close enough for her scent to entice him, but not close enough to touch. "I wanted you, and I…well, I didn't want to do anything that would ruin last night for us."

Stay in the moment. He now understood that she'd meant that as much for herself as for him.

"Sounds like the weekend's over already. What about visiting my folks in Nebraska?"

She lit up at the suggestion, but not the way he wanted. "You should go. I can travel back to Richmond and take care of business, and then we can meet again next Friday or Saturday and spend the weekend together."

"You're my wife, not my mistress. I wanted to show you off to the folks. Show you where I come from." Back to his roots. Back to a time before Al-Bazan and the nightmare he needed to forget.

"I can't right now. I'm sorry."

I'm sorry? How many times had he heard her say that this morning?

Becky seemed genuinely distressed. "I have to get back to Richmond and see my own parents tonight." She gestured to the laptop behind her. "And there's this emergency I need to handle."

"At work."

She propped her hands at her hips and puffed her sweet little self up into a defensive posture. "I may not be defending my country, but I do defend its citizens." Now she was sounding like a lawyer. "My job here is important, too."

"Didn't say it wasn't. Just that the timing sucks."

"Yes, well, you can't always predict when the

enemy will attack, can you? I can't always predict when one of my clients will need me."

Enemy? Poor choice of words. A gut-deep reaction to fire and flying metal, the acrid smell of sulfur in the air—screams, blood, senseless death—steamed inside him. His breath lodged in his chest. *"Watson! Fall back! Fall back!"*

Zachariah clenched his fists until his forearms ached, fighting off the memories before they could take hold.

"Zachariah?"

He jerked at the cool touch on his feverish skin and snapped his vision back into focus. Blond hair. Blue eyes. Becky's fingers on his chest.

"You left me again." Her husky voice and upturned face revealed real concern. *Hell.* Maybe Travis hadn't spooked her at all. Maybe *he* was only thing that could frighten Becky.

Shaking his arms loose at his sides, Zachariah retreated from her touch and forced himself to breathe in clean air tinged with her subtle, exotic perfume. He crooked the corner of his mouth into a reassuring grin. "Are we having our first fight?"

"No. I think we're getting a crash course on who we really are outside the bedroom." She reached out to him, moving slowly as though she expected him to freak out on her again. When he held his ground, she bravely moved forward and wrapped her arms around his waist, turning her cheek into the center of his chest. "I'm sorry I have to leave so soon. You should go visit your family. Relax. Enjoy them. I promise I'll be just as anxious to see you next time you come home as I was yesterday."

As humbled by her comfort as he was aware of her warmth softening against his body, Zachariah folded his arms around her and held her close. "I'm not ready to leave you again." He dipped his nose to the crown of her fragrant hair. Whatever she was dealing with— whatever mess he was bringing to the table—they could work past it. If they worked together. "How about we put Nebraska off until next week, and I come with you to Richmond and meet your family?"

"Meet…?" Bye-bye, warmth. Becky pulled away and returned to the desk in an almost insulting hurry. "No. It'd be boring. There's a party everyone's busy with—political stuff. You wouldn't know anyone. And I truly have to work on a case. I couldn't be with you all the time. Probably not much at all."

Perhaps he shouldn't blame her for developing this sudden prickle in her attitude. He must have scared her but good more than once since coming home. He wasn't the same prize a girl would want to take home to Mommy and Daddy that he'd been eighteen months ago.

Well, she needed to get over it. *He* needed to get over it. And that wasn't going to happen if they were hundreds of miles apart for a whole week. There had already been too much time and distance between them.

Just like that, his decision was made. Zachariah pulled his duffel bag off the closet shelf and tossed it onto the bed. He hoped his jeans and polo weren't too wrinkled up to meet the in-laws.

Clutching an official-looking file in her hand, Becky watched him organize his things and pack his bag. "What are you doing?"

Zachariah dropped his towel and pulled on a clean pair of boxers. "You told me you were a big girl yesterday. Well, I'm a big boy. I'm pretty good at making friends. I adapt well to different situations. I can occupy my time if you're busy—catch up on my sleep, hook up with some buddies, see the sights. Look, I know we're doing this whole relationship thing backward—we had a hell of a honeymoon eighteen months ago, then we got married, and now we're gettin' to know each other."

"That's just how it is for us. I don't mind—"

"I do." Zachariah shook out his jeans and pulled them on, well aware that those wheels were churning inside her head, thinking hard—thinking of excuses?—as she watched every movement. "Eventually, we're going to have to meet each other's folks. So why not now? We need to learn more about what we do with our lives, who we care about—outside this hotel room. I've only got a few weeks, darlin'. If I can't see you during the day, then I want to be there every night to talk about what's going on in your world and to welcome you home, not just to the bedroom."

The one place where it seemed they'd always known everything they needed to about each other.

"But I can be more efficient, and get everything done faster, if you're not there to distract me." A reasonable argument. But he wasn't buying it. "Besides, my mother isn't feeling well."

"Then I won't tire her out or expect her to entertain me." He pulled his billfold out of his camo pants and tucked it into his jeans. "Look, I promise to be my old, charming self, not that battle-fatigued monster you picked up at Quantico yesterday."

"Zachariah…"

"This isn't a debate, darlin'." He rolled up his uniform and stuffed it into the bag. "I'm coming with you."

5

WHEN BECKY PULLED UP TO the curb, she couldn't help
but check her rearview mirror to make sure the tan
SUV that had been behind her for the past two miles
drove on past.

With the glare from the afternoon sun reflecting off
its windshield, she couldn't make out the driver. The
same man who'd left messages in a tinny, mechanically altered voice on her answering machine at work?
The heavy breather on her home phone? Was it the
man who had dared to call her parents' house late last
night, asking for Becky and then hanging up on her
father when he'd taken the phone from her mother to
ask the caller to identify himself?

As the vehicle zipped on by, she wanted to believe
it was just a soccer dad, late to pick up his son or
daughter from practice. But little about her life seemed
that simple anymore.

Slowly releasing the breath she'd been holding,
Becky unclamped her fingers from the steering wheel
and shut off the engine. She sat there for several
minutes longer, baking in the July sun that blazed
through her windows, giving the SUV plenty of time

to circle the block, in case it wasn't a coincidence and the driver had been following her, after all—trying not to wish that she was still cocooned in bed with Zachariah wrapped possessively around her weary, well-loved body.

Maybe she shouldn't have been so eager to ditch her, *ahem, husband,* for the afternoon. She'd needed some time and space to think about the best way for her to proceed this week. Since he'd already dubbed her sporty little car the "sardine can," she'd suggested that he might enjoy a more comfortable ride down to Virginia's capital city if he got his pickup out of storage and drove himself.

But with his black truck riding her tail for two hours along Interstate 95 all the way to the parking lot of her downtown Richmond condo, it had been next to impossible to concentrate on work or her family. Instead of using the drive time to come up with a sensible plan, the web of half truths she'd created about her marriage—first to appease and then to protect her parents—had seemed stickier with every passing mile. How did she introduce a mystery husband she barely knew herself?

Hey, Mom and Dad, this is Zachariah. He's a hero home from a war zone. He's the most incredible lover I've ever had. But then, you don't want to hear that about your good little girl. Proper society women don't discuss such things.

Who is this mystery man, you ask? Well, I can't tell you much about him—though I suspect he's suffering from some kind of post-traumatic stress so he may get freaky on you at unexpected moments. Don't let his scars or size or the fact you haven't met three generations of his family scare you off. And, by the way—after I picked him up in a bar and slept with him, we snuck off to a justice of the peace and got married. Eighteen months ago. Never told you. Never told anyone.

"Surprise." Becky's stomach twisted into knots, just imagining the backlash if she laid out the whole truth. Right. That would go over real well.

With some kook sending hate mail and calling her almost every day now—even using her parents' unlisted number to try to harass her—Becky didn't need the publicity of suddenly announcing a political heiress's secret marriage to Captain America. Her pissed-off fan didn't need the tabloid fodder. Her parents didn't need to be wounded by the tawdry details. Zachariah didn't need to go to that awful place inside his head that made her think of a ticking bomb, ready to explode.

Still, there was a lot to be said for broad shoulders and that tough, don't-mess-with-me set to his jaw standing between her and the kooks in her world. But Zachariah had agreed to give her some time to deal with the business and family calls she'd received this morning. While she went to her office, met with a client and checked in on her parents, he was going to hook up with some Marine buddies in the area. Then they'd meet back at her condo for a late dinner. On a Sunday, there wouldn't be any suspicious mail delivered—and she hoped like hell that the dead flowers on her doorstep were a thing of the past.

She was praying they could get back to the business of their honeymoon for at least one more night. Maybe they'd discover that they could make magic in any bed. Or maybe they'd discover that sequestered away from reality was the only place their relationship worked.

"Don't go there, girl." Becky looked in the rearview mirror and chided herself. She needed to subtract her emotions from the equation and think logically.

Step one? Get out of the car and do her job. Don't let that anonymous creep's vile invective rattle her confidence. After all, messages like *"Hello, bitch. Where are you hiding? Don't think I can't find you. You can't deny me the things I want"* were just words. If the coward didn't have the balls to do more than talk tough, or even use his real voice, then she wasn't going to be intimidated.

She had more tangible dangers to worry about. Like Nick Cunningham's violating the restraining order Becky had filed to protect his ex-wife.

Since the tan SUV seemed to have disappeared, Becky decided she'd made it safely to her client's house in the Richmond suburb of Chesterfield. After cracking open the Nissan's windows, Becky climbed out. Through the mask of her dark sunglasses, she stole a moment to check up and down the sidewalk. She was in the heart of suburbia. Matching houses and young trees lined the street. Men mowed lawns, women chatted over fences and hedges, and children played in nearly every yard.

Except this one.

Becky turned to study the eerily quiet split-level

home with its profusion of deep red roses blooming against the pale gray siding. Dimitra Cunningham was an expert gardener who'd brought her skills to the U.S. when she'd emigrated from the Ukraine with her husband, American Nick Cunningham. After eight years of marriage, one bright, sensitive son, and constant intimidation and abuse, Dimitra had filed for divorce.

She'd gotten what she'd been able to afford on her own—cut-rate attorney Roger Sligh. Sligh had had enough complaints filed against him to limit his client list to a variety of petty criminals and desperate wives who thought *some* representation was better than no representation.

This wasn't the first of Roger Sligh's cases she'd had to clean up since going to work for the State. But it was by far the messiest.

Sligh should have argued that Dimitra had several American connections beyond her ex-husband—a design job with a florist, volunteering with her son's kindergarten class, working part-time as a translator with the State commerce office. But her ex's attorney had convinced the judge that Dimitra was a flight risk back to her homeland and, consequently, she'd been denied all but supervised visitation with her own son. While the scumbag ex had refused to pay his alimony, Dimitra had been let go from her State job and threatened with revocation of citizenship, deportation and loss of her home and her son.

That was when Becky had stepped into the picture.

She wouldn't put up with that kind of crap from any man, and she wouldn't let Dimitra put up with it, either.

Becky had secured her client's citizenship and her home, as well as custody of Nick, Jr. She'd filed all the paperwork to get mother and son the missing payments owed them, and they were waiting for a court appearance to seek further damages and to turn things around so Dimitra's ex would wind up with the supervised visitation rights.

Two days after Becky's first courtroom appearance against Nick Cunningham and his suddenly outmaneuvered lawyer was when the first anonymous letter had arrived.

Coincidence? *Ha!* As soon as she could prove Nicholas Cunningham, Sr., was behind the threats, she'd have him arrested.

But until she had the evidence she needed…? Becky glanced up and down the street one more time, making sure the driver of the tan SUV wasn't the threat she'd imagined.

With the strap of her leather attaché case tucked neatly over her shoulder, Becky circled her car and stepped over the curb into the yard. Though Dimitra's home looked as picture perfect as any other house on the street, inside the woman's haven had been violated. Her call this morning had been weepy but to the point.

A gasping sob and then, "I am sorry to call you on a Sunday, Ms. Owens. You said your cell was for emergencies only. But I could not reach anyone at your office, and—" she sniffed back another sob "—Nick… he was here last night. Nicky was gone to a friend's, thank God. But it is bad, Ms. Owens. He was so angry. What should I do?"

So much for a restraining order. Dimitra Cunningham had sounded like she needed more than an
attorney. The poor woman—kept isolated for years by
her husband—needed a friend. Following the curving
brick walkway up to the front door, Becky steeled
herself for anything and knocked.

A few moments passed before she heard movement
behind the door. Then she heard the slide of a chain, a
dead bolt and another lock being turned. When the door
opened, it seemed there was no one there. "Dimitra?"

Her client was hiding behind the door. Not a good
sign. "Come in, Ms. Owens."

When she'd first met the shy, dark-haired woman
in her office, Becky had been charmed at the way
Dimitra's accent turned Ms. into *Meez* and Nick into
Neek. But there was nothing charming about the warm,
muggy air inside the house, or the dark shadows from
which Dimitra appeared as she pushed the door shut
and locked it three times behind Becky.

"Are you hurt?" Becky asked. "Did Nick hurt you?"

Dimitra Cunningham was a couple of inches taller
than Becky's five feet, four inches. But with the way
the slender woman shook her bowed head, Becky felt
like a giantess. She wanted to reach out and comfort
her, but she wrapped both hands around the strap of her
bag and held on. Dimitra looked as though she might
break if anyone—even a well-meaning friend—
touched her right now.

"Why is it so hot and humid in here?" Becky asked,
while a quick once-over helped her verify that her
client didn't appear to have been physically harmed.

"Please." Dimitra gestured toward the living room and politely invited Becky to take a seat. She worked a wrinkled handkerchief between her hands as she followed Becky inside. "I woke at three in the morning to the sound of Nick's car driving away—I do not know how long he was here before that. I can't believe I slept so soundly. I suppose, with Nicky staying the night at his friend's for a birthday party, I was not so worried about keeping watch."

"Is Nicky safe?"

"Yes. The mother of his friend has agreed to keep him until I can fix things."

Perspiration beaded beneath the elastic waistband of Becky's skirt. "Like the air conditioning?"

"Yes. I think Nick did something to the unit outside—cut a pipe or turned off a switch." She perched on the sofa across from Becky. "And I do not want to open the windows because—"

"You're afraid he'll get in that way. Is that why the lights are out and the shades are drawn? So he can't tell that you're here?" Dimitra nodded. "Did you check the damage yourself? If it's just a switch, we can document that he was on the premises and then easily get the air turned back on. If he did some physical damage, we can call someone to fix it."

Dimitra's bottom lip quivered as she struggled to contain some emotion. Anger, Becky guessed—hoped—judging by the color staining her client's checks. Dimitra's dark brown eyes were too red-rimmed and bloodshot to have many tears left to shed. "I cannot go out there."

A bolt of alarm quickened Becky's pulse. "You said Nick has gone, right?"

Dimitra nodded. Her fingers nearly ripped the white handkerchief in two. "I have not been into my kitchen to prepare breakfast or lunch. I cannot go into the backyard. I cannot look out my windows or go into my garden to see it again."

Cannot sounded like something emotional rather than any physical barrier. Had Nick done something else besides cut off the A/C? Becky was already on her feet, on her way to the back door before Dimitra hurried after her.

She reached the back door off the kitchen, checked it for signs of forced entry, checked for graffiti on the windows—checked for a crude, folded-up note, slipped inside the door like the first ones she'd received.

When nothing more tangible than Dimitra's fearful reluctance to look outside spoke of danger, Becky unlocked the door and stepped out onto the deck. "That son of a bitch."

Though Dimitra turned away from the afternoon sunshine, Becky crossed straight to the railing and took in every vicious, deliberately hurtful detail. The backyard had been ruined. Dimitra's elaborate garden, with many of the blooms at the peak of their season, had been vandalized beyond what any anonymous culprit might do. Every flower had been beheaded or trampled underfoot. Every pot and piece of statuary had been shattered. A white trellis, covered with rose vines had been tipped over and hacked at with an ax or machete. Beyond the destruction of Dimitra's sanctuary—the garden she took such meticulous pride and joy in—the grass in the yard had been gouged up. Even Nicky's swing set had been attacked. It was bent into a shallow V across the top, and its swing dangled from a single chain.

"I am so sorry." Outraged by the violence before her, Becky didn't waste time with more inadequate apologies. She closed the door behind her and guided Dimitra back to the living room. "We need to have pictures taken of the damage. We'll call your insurance man and the police. I'll need this on record for our case."

Dimitra's steps slowed stubbornly. "You know it does no good. Even if the police come, they will say vandals did this. Teenagers. They will say I cannot prove Nick is responsible."

Becky halted beside her. "Did you see Nick out there last night? Are you sure it was his car driving away?"

"Who else would do this to us?"

"If you didn't see him, I can't have him arrested."

Dimitra's dark eyes widened like saucers. "It was dark outside, but I saw his car in front of the neighbor's house, speeding away in the middle of the night."

Becky had no doubts about who had done this, either, but Dimitra's testimony sounded weak, even to her. A good lawyer would easily pick apart her story. "Do you know what kind of vehicle Nick drives now?"

Please say black pickup truck.

With her suspicions about the calls and letters, Becky had the make and model memorized. Did Dimitra?

The other woman's hesitation gave away her answer. She couldn't make the positive ID. "Don't you believe me?"

"You know I do." She supposed Nick could have borrowed another vehicle easily enough. A tan SUV, perhaps? Hiding the shiver that ran down her back, Becky pried Dimitra from her handkerchief and squeezed her hand. "Don't worry. I'll call the police myself to report it." She pulled her cell phone from her bag. "You? Go pack some things for you and Nicky. We'll pick him up and then I'll take you both to a hotel. I don't want you staying here until we get that mess cleaned up, the air back on and some kind of security system installed."

Dimitra squeezed back. "Thank you, Ms. Owens. I didn't know who else to turn to. Thank you."

With a reassuring smile that wasn't quite as confident as she would like, Becky shooed Dimitra up the stairs and dialed the Richmond chief of police. When George Wesley answered, she swallowed her pride and identified herself. "That's right, Chief Wesley, I'm Bertram's daughter. I'm an attorney for the State now."

"I've known your father for thirty-some years. Call me George, not Chief." After a polite inquiry about her mother's health and a teasing reference to the days when "Old Bertie" had worked for the D.A.'s office, George had been a patrol officer and the two met in the same café for coffee, the police chief got serious. "So, what is it I can do for you?"

Even if it meant using her father's influence, Becky

was going to see that Dimitra got the help and protection she needed. "I'd like to talk to you about one of your officers, Nicholas Cunningham. I have reason to believe he's been terrorizing his ex-wife."

Becky relayed the details of the backyard destruction and gave the chief a brief history of Nick and Dimitra's disastrous marriage and punitive divorce. With a hearing on settlement and custody issues scheduled for later this week, his motive was obvious—punish Dimitra for taking a stand against him.

"She's afraid to report him to the local police. She believes they'll take his side."

"I can't make any guarantees, but I'll definitely look into it," Chief Wesley promised. "Say hi to your mother and father for me."

"I will. Thank you."

Becky disconnected the call and paced the foyer, waiting for Dimitra to finish packing. Though she'd helped more than one victim in the past year-and-half get the money or property a former spouse owed, she always had the antsy feeling that there was something more she could do. That was the Owens way, after all—find a cause, support it—become a part of it. Attack it with everything she had inside her, every tool she had at her disposal.

For her father it was politics. Supporting the right candidate, promoting his or her ideas, getting them elected to office, advising them to help create useful, effective leaders.

For Becky's mother, the cause had always been to support her husband. Though as the years passed, her influence—more on the issues than the politicians themselves—had become as valued and respected as her father's.

It was one hell of a legacy to live up to. Maybe it was that in-bred urge to be doing something more that left her feeling so trapped inside the locked doors and covered windows of Dimitra's house—as though she were a helpless victim, too, instead of the strong advocate her clients needed.

A glimpse of sunshine would snap her out of this nervous state. A breath of fresh air would be even better. Combing her fingers through her bangs to lift them off her sticky forehead, Becky unlocked the front door and pulled it open. She turned her face into the breezy sunshine pouring through the screen door, expecting to find relief.

But instead of blue sky, her gaze went straight to the bright white rectangle of paper tucked beneath the windshield wiper on the front of her car.

Her whole body tightened like a fist. "No. Not here. Not now."

Becky shoved the screen door open and darted onto the porch, desperately looking for someone, anyone, that didn't belong on this peaceful street. How had he found her? Was it Nick Cunningham? Was he still here? Or maybe this terror was the work of Dimitra's former lame-ass attorney, Roger Sligh. He couldn't make an ex-husband pay in court, but he'd have no problem going after the woman who was already appealing his fourth excuse for a case.

Up and down the block, little had changed. Men

worked in their yards. Children still played. Did they all belong? Was anything besides that envelope out of place?

Though a part of her wanted to duck back inside the house and lock the door, she needed answers more.

With a warning to Dimitra, Becky shut the door and hurried out to her car. The envelope was the same as the others. Crisp white. Her name was typed on the front with no return address or postmark. She glanced over each shoulder, but no one had paused a game to watch her, no one seemed curious enough to peek through a window. So Becky lifted the wiper blade and picked up the envelope.

As soon as she removed the pressure of the wiper, the envelope began to tick.

"Oh, my God." Becky jumped back, dropping the hated gift as if it had singed her fingers. "Oh, God."

She meant to run but froze with fear. With shock. With an increasing paranoia that had her looking from house to house, person to person.

Down at her feet the unsealed envelope had spilled its contents across the pavement. A watch without a band, sporting a shattered crystal now. The back had popped open and a battery had fallen out. The ticking had stopped. There was a small metal disk, about the size of a quarter, plus four colored wires—and the inevitable message, personalized just for her.

Becky squatted down and pulled the folded paper the rest of the way out of the envelope, smoothing it open across her lap. Even as the afternoon sun burnt into her fair skin, her blood ran cold.

I knew I'd get you to come to me, bitch. Do right by me or I'll have to teach you a lesson. Your time is running out.

"To Lance Corporal Darrell Watson."

"To Watson."

Zachariah raised his bottle and clinked it against the other two. "To Watson."

Then he tipped the icy bottle and swallowed a long draught of the tangy beer past the lump of emotion clogging his throat.

Lieutenants Thomas Murphy and Deke Stahlnecker had been in Al-Bazan with Zachariah. They'd been at the kid's memorial service, too, wearing their dress blues with new ribbons and service medals that matched Zachariah's.

But they hadn't held that kid in their arms. They hadn't watched him die.

Still, he might not be here now, drinking a toast to their fallen comrade, if blue-eyed Murphy hadn't flown in with the rescue chopper, and taciturn Deke hadn't laid down cover fire so their Spec Ops unit could load up and get the hell out of…hell.

The crowd around them at the Capitol Bar & Grille picked up as patrons began to arrive for dinner. But the three of them quietly sat at the high round table in the corner of the bar area for a few moments longer, letting the increasing buzz cocoon their bubble of silent respect.

But Murphy had never been able to stand the quiet for very long. He set down his bottle beside the empty one in front of him and laughed. "You two remember that waitress who had our table when we had that forty-eight-hour pass in Germany?"

Deke nodded. "Wiesbaden. November. Dagmar."

Zachariah didn't know whether he was grinnin' at Deke's aversion to lengthy sentences or the fact his memory never failed him. Maybe he was just grinnin' because sittin' with Ren and Stimpy here reminded him of times before Al-Bazan.

"Yeah." Murphy braced his elbows on the table and leaned forward to share a conspiratorial whisper. "Dagmar the *Hag*mar." He pointed his bottle toward Zachariah. "I swear to God, Captain, she could have taken you in a fight."

Zachariah nodded, remembering the size of the "gazongas" pushing at the top of her frilly white blouse, if not the face. "She needed horns on her helmet."

Murphy continued the trip down memory lane. "When I ordered that last round—"

"After seven mugs," Deke clarified.

"I thought she was gonna do me some mischief."

Mischief? How could a man not laugh when a New York Irishman, hardened by life on the streets and honed to be just as physically tough by the Corps, used a phrase like that? "Did Dagmar scare you, Murphy?"

The lieutenant leaned back, rattling his stool with a dramatic mock shiver. "Well, when she said she was gonna cut me off, I crossed my legs."

Even Deke's stocky shoulders shook with a laugh. "Too much woman for you, huh?"

"Too much woman for all three of us put together." Murphy raised his bottle to make another toast. "To Dagmar."

Zachariah shook his head while Deke and Murphy drank. He had plenty of woman waiting for him back at Becky's condo. No horns. Perfect breasts. Tough and sensible the way Dagmar had been, but feminine and soft and sexy in a way that had him checking his watch and wondering if it was too soon to hurry back to her place and christen the bed.

Or the kitchen table.

And maybe the living room floor if he couldn't get this itchy hunger to be with her out of his system.

But, no—it was 6:20. She'd said to give her until 7:00 p.m. to put out all the fires that had taken her away from their honeymoon long before he'd had his fill of her.

"He's lookin' at his watch again. Wondering if it's too soon to call." Murphy's smart-ass comment interrupted Zachariah's thoughts.

"Woman trouble," Deke agreed.

Zachariah took one final drink and plopped his bottle down on the table. "There's no trouble," he insisted, shrugging off their teasing. "Can I help it if I'd rather spend my time with a beautiful woman than with you two ugly yahoos?"

Murphy grabbed his heart. "I'm wounded. Deke's twice as ugly as I am."

"If I grew a pair of tits, you'd make a pass at me," Deke countered with his usual dry humor.

Murphy puckered his lips and blew him a kiss.

"Shut up."

Even with Deke's urging, the Irish chopper pilot couldn't keep his mouth shut. "She's that fine, is she, Captain?"

"Fine enough that I asked her to marry me."

"Whoa!" Murphy made a cross with his fingers and held them up near Zachariah's face. "You proposed?"

"And...sir?" Deke prompted.

Zachariah looked from man to man. Comrade to comrade. Friend to friend. He could trust them with this.

"We're married."

"Congratulations, sir."

"Why you sly old son of a bitch!" Murphy must have figured the curse wasn't catching. He smacked Zachariah's shoulder. "When did this happen?"

"Eighteen months ago."

Deke's nearly bald head wrinkled with thought. "Sir, we deployed eighteen months ago."

Zachariah nodded. "The ceremony took place the morning of the day we reported for duty."

"So you haven't had a honeymoon?"

Murphy threw up his hands. "Then what the hell are you doing here with us?"

"We promised to drink a toast to Corporal Watson."

"Done. Go." Deke, of course.

Murphy was more vocal. He pushed back his stool and stood. "Hell, Deke and I were gonna see if we could get some tail tonight—"

"We were going to see if we could meet some ladies."

"—but if we need to throw you a bachelor party—"

"Shut up, Murphy." Deke pulled out his wallet and

threw a bill onto the table. "Sir, it was good to see you. It was good to be stateside with you."

"I appreciate the hometown history lesson."

Deke climbed off the stool, standing not too much taller than he'd been sitting down. "Not a problem. I'd be glad to give you a tour any day." Was that a smile? "But not tonight. The drinks are on me, to celebrate the nuptials."

"Thanks."

"I'll keep an eye on Lieutenant Stud Man tonight. You go home to Mrs. Clark."

Mrs. Clark. Yeah. Was that the first time he'd heard it said out loud? Sounded weird. Sounded right.

Zachariah stood. "You can't give me an order, Lieutenant."

"No, sir."

"I'm out of here."

6

"MOM?" BECKY RAPPED SOFTLY against the painted door frame, wondering whether the soft strains of a Handel suite meant her mother was indulging a passion or if the lack of light in the bedroom meant she'd drifted off to sleep. "Are you awake?"

Giving her eyes a few moments to adjust to the shadows, Becky waited in the doorway for an answer.

"Becky?" She heard the whisper of silk sliding against silk, the soft thud of something hitting the rug, and a pair of clicks before the music abruptly stopped and the lamp beside the bed came on. Even at its lowest wattage, the light was shocking in the darkness. "Oh, sweetheart. Yes, come in. Come in."

Becky blinked her eyes into focus and saw her mother shielding herself from the light with one hand while she tried to fluff her pillows and push herself up to a sitting position with the other. "Here. Let me help."

Hurrying past the familiar decor of cream and gold French country furniture in what Lily Owens called her "resting room," Becky stooped beside the bed to pick up the glasses case that had fallen to the floor. She set it in her mother's lap, then reached behind her to prop the pillows upright and help her mother lean back against them.

Lily spared only a moment to tuck her silk robe up around her neck before stretching out her arms and welcoming Becky with a hug. "Come here."

Becky willingly bent down and wrapped her arms around her mother's fragile shoulders. "It's good to see you. I've missed you."

"Me, too." Lily's hold tightened with a surprising strength before she leaned back and patted the cream silk coverlet beside her. "Do you have a minute to chat? Or have I slept through your visit again?"

Becky smiled at the older woman, who was a slimmer, more delicate version of herself, right down to the blue eyes and straight, slightly upturned nose. Other than a few extra lines around her eyes and mouth, and the striking snow-white color of her hair as it returned and thickened after losing her golden locks to chemotherapy, they could be twins. They were certainly best friends.

Becky touched the canopy of filmy green silk that soared above the bed and slipped underneath it to sit on the edge. Curling one leg beneath her, she took one of her mother's elegant, if slightly bony now, hands in hers. "I'm later than I planned, getting away from the office, but I wanted to check in and see how you're doing."

"In your office on a Sunday?" Lily arched an eyebrow and clicked her tongue behind her teeth. "Did your father call you?"

"It's been a few days since I've been out to the house, and I wanted to see you." The eyebrow arched another notch. A partial mastectomy, chemo and radiation may have sapped her mother's strength, but nothing could dull that intuition. Becky laughed. Bertram Owens had been found out. "Okay. So he called. He was worried about you."

"He worries too much." Lily released her daughter to mark and close the book lying on the other side of her. "I must have fallen asleep reading again. I suppose your father turned out the light." She set the book on the bedside table beside the CD player and laid her glasses on top. "Not that I don't appreciate relaxing with a good romance, but I swear I'm going to go stark, raving crazy if he doesn't let me out of this bed to do something more invigorating than read and sleep all day long."

"I thought your quarterly follow-up shot knocked you flat. The last one did."

Lily nodded with a sigh. "True. They do. I was at the oncologist's to get my shot on Wednesday and I slept almost all day Thursday. But by Friday afternoon I was ready to go for a walk or shop for the linens I want to use for Senator Barclay's reception next Saturday. I know I'm not yet able to go full tilt all day long like I used to. But your father won't even let me sit down and go over the menu with the caterer."

The press and two generations of politicians liked to talk about what a steel-spined curmudgeon her father was, but Becky knew where her own stubbornness really came from. "Mom, Dad has been married to you for thirty-five years. We thought we were going to lose you last year. Don't give him too much grief for wanting to keep you around a good while longer."

"I know he loves me. And I love him. Never doubt that, my dear." She smoothed her fingers through her elegantly short hair. "But the cancer has been gone for six months. Everything is healing the way it's supposed to. I do what the doctors tell me. I eat well, take my meds, keep every appointment." She reached over and gave Becky's hand a light squeeze. "I have my family's prayers and support. But part of my ongoing recovery should include my mental health, as well. Bertram's heart may be in the right place, but he can't keep doing every little thing for me, or shield me from the outside world. If he's not careful he'll overdo it, and then he'll be the one in the hospital."

Becky frowned. "Nothing's wrong with Dad, is it?"

A hint of concern deepened the lines beside Lily's mouth. "Just some marginally high blood pressure. The doctor says it's stress-related, which probably means me."

Stress? High blood pressure? One more reason surprising her parents with news of her marriage to Zachariah wasn't the best idea. Even if her mother was feeling stronger, as she insisted, she still looked small and fragile in this big bed. Even if she could physically handle a big announcement, she'd nonetheless be hurt that Becky hadn't confided the news to her sooner.

"…doesn't even like for me to answer the stupid telephone. Hello? Earth to Becky?"

Becky jerked her chin up, wondering how long she'd been staring at the spine of that book. "I'm sorry. What were you saying about a phone call?" *The* phone call? Becky pulled her leg from beneath her and sat up straight. "Dad said someone from my office called you? It wasn't my assistant, Cheryl, was it?"

The matching blue eyes were frowning. "No, I'd recognize her voice. She's always so professional— she identifies herself right away. Though I didn't get to say two words before your father picked up the line and told me to hang up. Beyond that…"

"So the caller didn't say anything to upset you?"

"Your father upset me. I can answer the phone and take a message."

"Was it a man who called?"

"I'm not sure."

"Was there anything…weird…about his voice?" Did it sound like a TV robot? Threaten payback? Ask for the *bitch?*

"Like I said, I really didn't get to speak to him." Her mother shifted closer on the bed. "Is there something wrong, sweetheart?"

"Wrong?" she mimicked, as if she were the small girl who'd once broken a vase while dancing through the house, not the grown woman who was doing everything she could think of to keep from breaking her parents' hearts. For half a second, she wanted to be that little girl again. She wanted to rewind the clock to a time when she didn't have to worry about ugly notes and abused clients and secret husbands.

But winding back the clock would mean no Zachariah. No perfect passion. No feeling beautiful and sexy and right in her skin, just from the look one particular man could give her.

"Becky Lynn Owens."

All three names. *Snap out of it!* If she stewed about things too much longer, her mother would definitely worry that all was not well in Beckyland.

Becky gathered her composure. She smoothed her skirt and stood with the serene smile she'd also inherited from her mother. "It's nothing, Mom. I'm just a little tired." That, at least was true. Spending any length of time with Zachariah tended to leave her exhausted. Happy. Satisfied. But exhausted. "If I'd known I had to go into work this afternoon, I'd have gotten more sleep last night."

"So what was keeping you up so late? Or should I ask whom?"

"I was…" Her hopeful smile faded as Becky hesitated.

Lily folded her arms across her chest and tilted her chin. Her eyes analyzed Becky's everything's-hunky-dory expression. "You know, dear, there's nothing you can't tell me. It seems like something's weighing heavy on your mind. It's not me, is it?"

"No. No more than I usually worry about the people I love."

"Uh-huh." Her mother wasn't completely buying her argument. "I may not be a hundred percent, and Bertram may worry like a mother hen when I try to get out of bed, but my ears work just fine. Is it man trouble? Lack of a man?"

"Mom!"

"Is it your job? I know State workers aren't always properly compensated for the hours and stress they put into their work. And you've yet to use your trust fund."

"It's not money."

Lily searched her daughter's face for answers. "Whatever it is, I'm always here to listen to you."

"I know. It's just something I need to work through for myself. Okay? You don't need to worry."

"I'm a mother. I can't help it."

Becky leaned in and traded another hug, holding on a little longer since she wasn't sure she should squeeze any harder. "I love you."

"I love you, too."

The instant she felt her mother's arms begin to weaken, Becky pulled away. Yet even though she sank back into the pillows as if she was growing weary, Lily's eyes continued to assess. "I feel that you're torn in a dozen different directions, dear. This *is* about a man, isn't it?" Lily yawned. "Is that why you asked about that call? Were you hoping someone special was trying to find you? Is it that man whose work takes him away from you so often?"

Becky pressed her lips together, silencing the gasp in her throat. She waited to speak until she was sure she could get the words out with a teasing smile. "You're scary, sometimes, Mom. I'll handle my own man trouble myself, though. Thanks." She kissed her mother's forehead, then reached over and turned out the light. "Good night."

"There are dozens of good men in this world for every bad one. If a good one loves you, you grab him and hold on tight. That's why I married your father. Didn't want him to get away." Her mother's sleepy voice followed her through the shadows as Becky tiptoed back to the hallway. "He's going to ask you to help with the senator's reception, by the way. You should invite that mystery man of yours to come if he's in town. I'd like to meet him and see if he's worth you putting your life on hold for him."

"DID YOU SAY GOOD-NIGHT TO your mother?"

Bertram Owens pulled off his reading glasses and waited for Becky at the bottom of the grand staircase that led from the second floor down to the marbled entryway of their riverside estate on the outskirts of Richmond. She smiled and kissed his cheek. "Yes. We chatted for a while and I gave her a hug. She was nodding off when I slipped out of the room."

"Did you discuss that phone call?"

She brushed a lock of salt-and-pepper hair off his forehead and nodded. "I don't think she was as upset as you thought. Still, I reassured her it was nothing to be concerned about. To be honest, she's more worried about you."

He scoffed.

"Mom thinks you're doing too much for her. Maybe at the expense of your own health?"

"It was a one-time fluctuation in my blood pressure. I'm fine."

"She will be, too." In fact, Lily Owens was probably further along in her recovery than Bertram gave her credit for. But Becky understood how impossible it was *not* to make sacrifices for the people you loved. "I, for one, however, am not afraid to admit I'm pooped. Now that I'm sure everything's cool here, I'm heading back into the city."

Back to her condo and the husband she was hiding there.

Was *he* the kind of good man her mother was talking about? What would her mother do if she really brought Zachariah to the reception and introduced him as the man in her life? With his long absences and recent mood swings, would Lily think Zachariah was a man worth twisting her life into knots over?

Maybe she could forestall the inevitable revelations of all her secrets and the consequences that would surely follow by distracting Zachariah with some I'm-sorry-I-missed-dinner sex. Becky grinned as she strolled past her father. She'd purchased a brand-new mattress and box springs to go on her antique four-poster just last month. Zachariah could help her test just how sturdy the new bed was.

Becky picked up her purse from the credenza near the front door. She looked through the beveled glass lining either side of the door and saw the orange and pink sunset turning the sky to dusk. *Damn.* Better make that I'm-sorry-I-missed-our-whole-evening-together sex. She'd phoned him earlier and warned him she'd be late and to go ahead and find something to eat on his own. Once she got out to her car, she'd better call him again. See if she could bring him a bottle of wine or some ice cream—or her own willing body—to help with her apology.

"Good night, Dad."

Stubbornness she might have inherited from her mom, but asking questions was a gift from her dad.

"I got an interesting call from George Wesley this

evening." Her father's low-pitched voice stopped her at the door. "Are you going to tell me what's going on?"

So close to escape. And yet so far.

Relaxing the telling pinch of her bottom lip between her teeth, Becky turned. "Sorry, Dad. It's work-related. I can't discuss it."

Bertram slid his fingers into the pockets of his charcoal slacks and relaxed his stance. "George seemed to think you were in some kind of trouble."

"There's a woman I'm defending who's in trouble. Chief Wesley is looking into something for me in regard to her case. I confess, I dropped your name so that he'd take my call at home on a Sunday afternoon."

"George will do right by you if he can." Instead of looking pleased that Becky had allowed his influence to be of even that much use to her, her father's brow knitted with a frown. "I asked Frederick to open a bottle of wine for me in the study. Care to join your old man for a nightcap before you go?"

The Owenses' butler had placed drinks in her father's study almost every night of the twelve years he'd worked for the family. Tonight was nothing special. "I better not, Dad. I haven't eaten dinner yet."

"Frederick can fix you something."

"No, thanks. I'm meeting someone in town."

"Who? It's not Peter Cass, is it? The new partner at Jaffrey, MacDougal, Wyndham and Cass? Arthur Mac-Dougal said you and Peter seemed to really hit it off when you interviewed with them."

That meeting had taken place more than a year ago. Even though she loved her job with the State, she'd interviewed for the position at the Richmond law firm to humor her father, who'd been spending most of his time at the hospital and had needed some humoring back then. But the job hadn't interested her, and neither had Peter. "No, Dad. Peter is nice enough, but he didn't exactly flip my switch if you know what I mean."

Her father winced at her choice of words. "There's more to a relationship than having your switches flipped." Sage advice from a man who'd made his marriage last. Maybe it was advice she should take to heart with Zachariah? "So, who are you meeting?"

"A friend. You don't know him."

"Him?" The eyebrows arched. "Is your beau state-side again?"

Busted.

She couldn't let one word slip around the master. So she used one of his own tricks against him—show how much he meant to her so he wouldn't mind if she changed the topic. Linking her arm through her father's, Becky gestured toward the black doors leading to his study. "All right. One drink. I can tell something's on your mind because you keep pestering me with questions. It's not Mom, is it? She said she was initially feeling tired from her last round of medication, but that she's rearing to get back to her life now."

Bertram patted her hand on his arm and walked her into the study. "I know. Her six-month checkup went just fine. There's been no recurrence of the cancer. Her PSA count continues to drop. But she still needs her rest."

Becky took a seat on the black leather sofa while her father poured her a glass of merlot. Once upon a time she'd curled up in his study to eat cookies and drink milk while he worked, but she knew there'd be nothing quite so benign about this particular father-daughter time.

She accepted the glass, took a sip of the deep, rich liquid and waited. "Well?"

He swirled and sniffed his glass before taking a drink. "When your assistant called Saturday morning looking for you, I didn't think much of it. I assumed you simply had your cell phone turned off."

"I did." She hadn't wanted anything to interrupt her reunion with Zachariah.

"And then this man called last night." *Ah.* Let the real inquisition begin. The wine in her mouth soured. "I thought your mother had already gone to bed."

"She told me she was still up, reading."

He nodded. "I think it's unusual that he never identified himself. Lily said the caller ID was similar to your work number—thought it might be a coworker. That's why she picked it up."

A coworker? No way. Her mother hadn't mentioned that. "Do you still have the number?"

"I called it back and all I got was an out-of-order signal. If he hadn't asked specifically for you, I would have dismissed it as a wrong number. Our caller ID box must be faulty. I'm having security replace it tomorrow morning." He sat on the sofa on the opposite side of the coffee table from her, and paused long enough to adjust his slacks and the unbuttoned collar of his oxford shirt before continuing. "I called you this morning because your mother was worried that she'd bungled some work-related message for you, and I didn't want her to have that stress."

"She shouldn't. I'm glad you called." Becky set her goblet on the table between them. She'd have to explain this next question, but she needed to know. "Mom didn't remember much about the caller. But you were on the line longer. Was the voice on the phone mechanically altered?"

"No. Did you expect it to be?"

"You're sure it was a man's voice?"

"Yes."

"But you didn't recognize it?"

"No." Bertram leaned forward, bracing his elbows on his knees. "Your visit tonight will appease your mother's concerns. But I expect you to tell me exactly what's going on. First your own staff can't locate you, and now you're talking about mechanically altered voices?"

Better give him at least a little bit of the truth and let him know she had the problem under control, or Daddy would be rallying the troops to protect her at the expense of her clients. "I didn't say anything to Mom, but I've gotten a couple of threatening phone calls. Most likely related to a case I'm working on."

"The one you talked to George Wesley about?"

"Possibly. I've reported everything to my supervisor and the police. I've taken all the security precautions I'm supposed to."

"Is someone trying to get you to quit the case?"

"The threats aren't specific, but that'd be my guess."

"And you haven't quit yet?"

"I won't. My client needs me."

"Good. I don't want to hear of any Owens quitting anything. Not your mother and her treatments. Not you and your work."

Becky could only stare while he got up to refill his glass. "You *are* Bertram Owens, right? I thought you wanted me to join a partnership, not defend misrepresented women and children on behalf of the State. You've always said my job didn't pay me what I'm worth and that my clients wouldn't appreciate me. And now you don't want me to quit? Why aren't you trying to smooth things out for me?"

"You said you've taken the necessary precautions."

This was too easy. "I have."

"Good." He kissed her forehead before returning to his seat. "If you do need me to step in, say the word, and I'll put in a call to Oliver Sherwood."

"Dad—he's the State Attorney General."

"He's your boss, isn't he?"

"A dozen times removed. He doesn't mess with cases like mine or deal with crank phone calls."

"He will if I ask him to. Should I?"

"No." Becky picked up her goblet and returned it to the bar sink. "I mean, I thought you would as soon as you heard about the calls, but I want to take care of this myself. I *can* take care of this myself."

"Of course, you can. You'll be fine."

Becky dumped the drink she hadn't really wanted and turned to face him. "Okay, what's going on here? The father I grew up with would already be poking his nose into my business, even if I asked him not to.

You're standing on the sidelines, acting like you're okay with everything I'm telling you."

He stood. "Make no mistake, I will do whatever is necessary to protect your mother. Until she's stronger, I intend to shield her from the stresses of my work, and I will shield her from yours, as well."

Becky tipped her chin, standing as tall as her height would allow. "I didn't tell her about the calls. I'm protecting her, too."

"I know." He made a placating motion with his hand. "Listen, I'm trying to take to heart the eloquent speeches you've given me on more than one occasion—about being an independent woman who wants to make her own way in the world."

"And…?" There had to be more.

"And, if you're strong enough to stand up to me and be your own person, see to your own safety, take care of your clients, then you're strong enough to do your old man a favor."

Becky laughed at his sheepish smile. She knew there had to be a catch to Bertram Owens's reining in his desire to control the lives of the people around him. "Now we're getting to what this meeting is really about. This has something to do with that fund-raising party next Saturday, doesn't it?"

He stretched his arms out to either side. "Guilty as charged. Though I'd be willing to postpone or cancel it, your mother is most insistent that we carry on. We're raising money for Ralph Barclay's reelection campaign to the Senate."

"And Senator Barclay has been an avid supporter of

funding for breast cancer research, and mammograms and treatment for women without insurance. I know those programs are important to Mom."

"It's her pet project. The reception is extremely important to her. She's been pushing herself too hard to make it come together, and that's probably why she's having such a hard time getting her energy back to normal this time."

She knew where this was going. Becky finally realized that her father wasn't above trading one consideration for another. He'd back off from fixing what he thought was wrong in her life if she rewarded his efforts by helping her mother. "Dad—"

"I'm determined that Lily take the week off to rest. The reception will be here at the house. She could still attend if she feels up to it, but you and I would take over the last-minute details, such as coordinating with the event planner and Barclay's campaign manager, and following up on the guest list."

Becky crossed the room. She'd been played. She didn't like it, but she had an idea that she was already on the losing end of this argument. "You mean 'you and I' as in mostly me taking over this party?"

"You'd make a beautiful hostess. And I know you can work a room the way your mother does to ensure we get generous contributions."

"I hate all that schmoozing."

"But you love your mother."

"Not fair, Dad." She had asked her assistant, Cheryl, to clear as much of her calendar this week as possible. But Becky had wanted the time to prepare for the Cunningham case. And if there should be a few moments left, to spend a little extra time with Zachariah. "That would mean some late nights. And a lot of travel from work to my condo to here and back."

The protest sounded weak, even to her own ears.

Bertram Owens, a cutthroat negotiator himself, jumped on the opening she gave him. "Then just stay here. You know we always keep your old room ready for you. Other than a few phone calls and a lunch meeting or two, anything you'd need to take care of for the party could be handled after hours."

Zachariah had already laid claim to her after-hours time. "What about my social life?"

"Well, since this jet-setting boyfriend of yours is out of town—again—I assumed you'd be free." He dropped an arm around her shoulders and hugged her to his side. "A man who leaves you alone for this long isn't giving you the attention you deserve, if you ask my opinion."

"I didn't." He let her pull away and she went to retrieve her bag.

Bertram polished off his drink. "James Enderle is working with Senator Barclay now. Did you know that?"

"I'd heard."

"Managing his campaign. I'm sure he'll become Barclay's advisor once he wins reelection. Hell, with his ambition, I imagine he'll be a senator himself one day. He was working very closely with your mother on this reception. The Enderles are good people."

"I know."

"If you take over the hostess duties, it'd be a chance for you and James to reconnect."

She'd stopped connecting with James Enderle after the third month of dating the M.I.T. honors graduate. As the son of one of her father's college fraternity brothers, he ranked high on her parents' list of prospective husbands. But James had proved to be more interested in the family name than in the family's daughter. And though he had enough charm to seduce an entire room of political supporters, he kissed like a cold fish and made love like a colder one.

Becky had known there was something more for her out there. Zachariah Clark was something more.

"I'm not interested in James."

"He always asks about you."

"Stop matchmaking, Dad. We're just friends. I'll work with him, but…" She looped her bag over her shoulder and shrugged. "What about the crank calls I've been getting? What if they affect the success of this party? Do you want to risk that?"

"You said you'd hired security."

Not exactly. "I said I'd taken care of it."

A quiet knock on the study door interrupted them. The gray-haired butler acknowledged Becky before turning to her father. "Good evening, miss. Sir, there's a Zachariah Clark at the front door."

Here? This front door? The blood drained from her head to her toes. *How…?*

"I don't know any Zachariah," her father answered.

"He's here to see Miss Becky, sir."

"Oh?"

Oh, no. "Thank you, Frederick. I have to go, Dad. Love you." She was already rushing toward the door.

"I love you, too, sweetheart. But who is this man?"

Um, that would be him. Becky skidded to a halt as Zachariah suddenly appeared behind Frederick. His broad shoulders filled the doorway and the guarded suspicion tightening his jaw filled the entire room.

How had he announced himself? *"I'm Becky's husband. What do you mean you've never heard of me?"* or *"I'm your daughter's secret lover and she's late for our latest tryst. Seen her around?"*

Apparently, he'd said something to connect them together, or else he'd simply ignored social protocol and had followed Frederick in to locate her for himself. "So this is where the party is," he drawled. "When you didn't show up when you said you would, I got worried. You leave a hard trail, woman. I've been all over town trackin' you down."

She tried to read those narrowed green eyes. Was that genuine relief at finding her that colored his voice? Or sarcasm?

"Becky?" As Frederick dismissed himself from the room, Bertram walked up behind her and curled a protective hand over her shoulder, pulling her back toward him. "Who is this man? He doesn't have anything to do with those crank phone calls, does he?"

Becky's stomach flip-flopped and she wanted to sink into the polished pecan wood floor. *Thanks for mentioning that, Dad. Let's alert the Marine Corps.* This was not the kind of stress Zachariah needed right now. "No, he doesn't."

"Crank phone calls?"

She could feel Zachariah's gaze on her, but her father answered. "If you're part of her security detail, I insist you get all the facts so you can protect her properly. Whom do you work for? What kind of arrangements have been made?"

Zachariah's long, silent exhale warmed her cheek with its telling pause. "I'm afraid there's been a mistake, sir. I'm with the United States Marine Corps. I'm on leave right now."

"Oh." Maybe she could crawl beneath the floorboards before her father pieced together the truth. "So you're working independently?"

"Right now, spending time with your daughter is the only work I'm interested in. I'm Zachariah Clark." He extended his hand and grinned.

Trapped between her father and the husband she knew so little about, Becky tilted her chin and sent every silent plea in her arsenal, begging Zachariah to turn around and walk away. *Please, please, please!* "I'm sorry you had to drive out all this way to find me. We can discuss things once we get back to town."

Her father surprised her by reaching around her to shake Zachariah's hand. "Bertram Owens. I like that kind of dedication. So you're taking good care of my daughter, Mr. Clark?"

"I'm doin' my best. As good as she'll let me."

Oh, no. They were bonding. Maybe under false pretenses, but there seemed to be some sort of mutual respect already forming between the two men.

"Yes, well, she can be a bit headstrong."

"You think?"

Apparently, that bond excluded her. "Hello, I'm right here. Quit talking about me."

The two men shared a chuckle.

She almost reached for Zachariah, almost touched him to demand he acknowledge her unspoken messages before he said something that would give them away. Lying to her parents about him wasn't the most noble thing she'd ever done, but her reasons were good. She needed an opportunity to convince him of that so he would understand—and hopefully forgive—the lie.

But at the last second, Becky curled her fingers into her palm. Why she had the right to touch the big, strapping stranger in her father's study would be something else she'd have to explain. "It's time to leave, yes?"

"Now that I'm here with you, there's no rush."

Zachariah's gaze swept over her upturned face. *Oh, crap.* He knew damn well how uncomfortable she was to have him here—how he'd caught her off guard by showing up out of the blue. He'd received every silent signal she'd sent his way, and was playing along with her urgings to keep his comments as brief as possible. But whether he was doing her a favor or giving her father time to reveal information that she hadn't yet, she couldn't tell.

Bertram crossed his arms and puffed up behind her. "You certainly look capable enough. This isn't your usual attire for work, though, is it?"

Faded jeans hugged Zachariah's thighs and hips like a softly worn glove and did wonderful things to show how powerfully he was built. The weathered green polo shirt he wore emphasized the color of his eyes. While Becky could appreciate those particular details, they would do little to impress her father.

"No, sir."

"If you're going to be on hand for next Saturday's party, I'll expect to see you in a tuxedo."

"A party Saturday?" Zachariah nodded. "I'll find something appropriate."

"Very good. You don't want to keep my daughter waiting."

"No, sir."

Thank God, the torture was ending.

"Good night, Dad." Becky stretched up on tiptoe to kiss her father and scooted around Zachariah into the foyer, hoping he'd take the hint and follow just as quickly. But the big guy refused to budge. "Zachariah?"

He turned and winked at her before shaking hands with her father again. "Nice to meet you, sir."

"Good night, Mr. Clark."

Zachariah retreated one step and then another. Once they were out of sight of the study, Becky grabbed his arm and tugged him out the front door.

"Thank you. I know that was awkward and I have some explaining to do, but thank you for not saying anything about us to Dad." As she released him and trotted down the steps to where her car and his truck were parked, she could sense that her thanks were hitting a wall of slow-brewing anger. *Keep moving. Keep talking.* "How did you find my parents' house? They're not exactly on Richmond's main drag."

He followed at a slower, more deliberate pace.

"Finding things is half of what I do for the Corps. Your family is pretty well known around town, I discovered. I can ask a few questions and read a map."

"I see." She dug her keys from her bag. "Well, what about your friends? I thought you were spending the day with them."

"It's after nine o'clock, Becky." He walked past his truck and followed her to her car. "I did grab a beer and some burgers with Murphy and Stahlnecker. But I left them two hours ago. They wanted to hit the bar scene tonight. I figured having an old *married* man tagging along would cramp their style."

Oy. Maybe she should stop talking before she made this tension between them any worse. She unlocked her car door and tossed her bag across to the passenger seat. "Okay, Mr. Map-Reader. Can you find your way back to my apartment on your own? Or do you need to follow me?"

Becky climbed in behind the wheel. But when she reached out to close the door, a big arm braced it open. A bigger body filled the gap between her car and the door and leaned in. "Cut the chitchat, Beckster, and answer two questions for me. Your father doesn't know you're married, does he?

"And why the hell do you need a bodyguard?"

7

BECKY PULLED HER KEY FROM the lock and opened the door to her condominium apartment. "He didn't exactly say he thought you were my bodyguard."

Zachariah walked in right behind her, close enough for her to feel the heat off his body if not the man himself. Just a shade closer than his black truck had followed behind her all the way home from her parents' house. At least he'd agreed to let her get home and beyond the hearing of curious strangers before answering his questions.

"Crank calls. Security assignments. Workin' a party. Protect you properly." He blocked her path to the door and locked the knob and security chain himself before turning and glaring down at her. "Why does your father think I'm some security guy you hired and not your husband?"

"It's complicated." A heavy sigh that was half fatigue, half frustration whooshed between her teeth. She tossed her attaché case onto the kitchen table and toed off her sandals. She needed sleep. She needed peace. She needed a few quiet minutes to think.

As she headed down the carpeted hallway toward

her bedroom, Zachariah carried one of her kitchen chairs to the front door and wedged it beneath the knob. "You think I'm too stupid to understand why you're embarrassed to tell your family about me? About us?"

"What?" She turned. Like she'd date—correction, marry—a stupid man. "I'm not embarrassed."

Now he was checking the windows above the tapestry couch in her living room. "So I'm married to a chronic liar?"

"Zachariah—"

"Maybe if you talk nice and slow and use little words, the big galoot will be able to figure out what's going on here."

"Don't blame me. Dad's the one who assumed you were a bodyguard."

"And you didn't correct him." Zachariah propped his hands at his hips, spreading his arms and shoulders in a stance that impossibly made him seem bigger and broader. "I told people we were married. Travis McCormick. Friends from my unit. I e-mailed my parents and told them I'd met someone special. A city girl. An attorney. A lady with real class."

"But not that you'd married me?"

"Don't look so relieved. My folks don't run in the same social circles as yours, so I'm sure the news that you and I are an item hasn't gotten back to 'Daddy' yet." His sarcasm stung. Intimating she and her family were snobs hurt, too.

"I didn't tell my parents that we eloped because I wanted to protect them."

"Gettin' married to me was bad news, huh?"

"Getting married, period, is the problem." Becky mirrored his stance, matching him in attitude if not size. "Our affair was the first—*most*—impulsive thing I have ever done in my life. Here was this big hunk of man who *got* the woman I was. The woman I am. I wasn't too fat, too smart, too rich, too bossy. You weren't intimidated by me, and you didn't want anything from me *but* me. How could I resist that?"

"An *affair?* You and I signed a marriage license, darlin'."

Becky could sling her own arrows, too. "Right. We're *so* married that you disappeared for months without a single word."

"I was on a mission. We weren't allowed to make outside contact so that our location wasn't compromised."

"You apparently found a way to e-mail your parents. And Travis."

He scraped his palm over the top of his head before squeezing his hands into fists and shaking the air. "*After* the blackout period. As soon as I could get to a computer, I e-mailed you, too."

"Three months, Zachariah. I waited three months."

His hand settled at the scruff of evening beard on his jaw. "That's the way a special operations unit works. Sometimes we're gone for a weekend—sometimes, it's eighteen months. Usually, we get advance notice as to when we're shippin' out, but sometimes, the colonel just calls and we go. When I'm deployed, I can't guarantee when I can pick up the phone and give you a call. You have to know what it's like to be married to a Marine."

"Well, I don't. I was alone. I needed to talk to you but I didn't know how to reach you until you sent that first message. Apparently, that's part of that newlywed training you conveniently forgot to tell me—" she sniffed "—about."

Oh, my God. Was she going to cry? Becky quickly turned her head and blinked away the grit stinging her eyes. She refused to let any emotion get the better of her. She needed to keep this discussion rational and focused.

"Darlin', I'm sorry. I didn't know you were worried…. I didn't know you were feelin' like that." The atmosphere in her living room changed in a heart-beat, as though the angry tension that had arced between them had been shot down out of the sky. Zachariah's posture softened; he seemed to take up less space. He took a step toward her, reached for her.

But Becky hugged her arms around her waist and backed away. Touching would be bad right now. Touching would make those tears fall. His hand fell back to his side and he held his ground.

"I'm sorry." His apology was a low-pitched rumble in his throat.

Becky nodded, feeling too spent to do more to ac-knowledge a regret that probably matched her own. Her voice was quiet when she finally spoke, but she articu-lated every word that had festered in her conscience for months now. "If I had been able to contact you back then, I would have told you that my mother went in for her annual exam the same January we were married. The doctor discovered a lump. And after mammograms and sonograms and biopsies, she was diagnosed with cancer."

"Ah, geez. You should have said something sooner."

"I'm saying it now, okay?" That square jaw nodded. "I'm an only child. Social events and big celebrations have always been very important to my parents. Maybe it has to do with generations of being socially and politically prominent, maybe it's because they couldn't have any other children and so they…spoil me."

Zachariah retreated to the couch and sat, making himself seem less like an adversary and more like a…friend. It was a weird concept to process through her brain when she'd always thought of him as her lover—one she might be desperately addicted to, but a lover all the same. Perhaps, if she could get to know him, learn to trust him as a friend as well as the perfect bedroom partner for her, then maybe the term *husband* could become more than just a word on a piece of paper.

"Is your mother gonna be okay?" he asked.

Becky nodded. "Regular self-exams and checkups are something she'll have to be faithful about the rest of her life, in case it comes back. But the surgeon removed the cancerous tissue and she's had chemo and radiation to help make sure it's completely gone and doesn't recur. Still, there's always a chance it could start growing somewhere else in her breasts or body."

"If she's half as strong as you, your mom will get through it just fine."

Zachariah's rugged face looked so calm, so matter-of-fact, that Becky felt a warm reassurance easing through her, quieting her inside. The idea of being comforted seemed at odds with the stiff upper lip that she'd maintained for eighteen long months. Yet accepting Zachariah's comfort was so tempting that she wanted to crawl into his lap and feel his arms around her. She wanted to sink into the strength that was greater than her own. But then she'd probably do something lame, such as cry.

And her problems were too far from being resolved to risk surrendering her own strength.

Curling her toes into the dark mauve carpet, Becky finished her confession from where she stood. "At any rate, to sum it all up, I didn't tell my parents about us because Mom has always talked about giving me this big, grandiose wedding. The social event of the season, the most important party she would ever plan. And here I'd already run off and gotten married—to someone they didn't even know. If the shock didn't set back her recovery, then knowing I cheated her out of that dream wedding probably would."

"And now that she's recovering?"

"She's better. She has really good days, but some bad ones, too. She's still not that strong. And my dad would do anything to protect her. I don't want my keeping us a secret from her to be a burden on him, either." Taking the first full breath she'd had since walking through the front door, Becky walked into the kitchen and pulled out a bag of chips from a cupboard and opened the fridge to find items to make sandwiches for them. She strengthened her voice to carry through the open archway over the counter between the living room and kitchen. "Now the lie has been going on for so long, it'd be even more of a shock and disappointment. How do I tell them without hurting them?"

"The same way you're telling me." Zachariah's voice, coming from the other side of the refrigerator door, startled her.

He'd followed her again.

Becky closed the door, offered up a thanks-but-it's-not-that-easy smile, plopped the loaf of bread in his hands and put him to work.

Their sandwiches were digesting in their stomachs before Zachariah brought up the other secret she'd worked so hard to keep to herself. "How much do your parents know about these phone calls?"

Becky took the plate he handed her and loaded it into the dishwasher. "Dad intercepted a call this weekend when Joe Stalker—that's what I've dubbed him—called the house, trying to find me. It's the first Dad has heard about them. I confirmed that I'd received a couple of disturbing calls."

"But it's been more than a couple, hasn't it?"

Becky nodded. "We decided not to tell Mom. I don't like her worrying about me. And she'd sense it if he knew something worse was happening to me."

"Would having a bodyguard around alleviate that worry?"

"I suppose." His fingers brushed against hers when he handed her their dirty glasses and Becky shivered at the contact. He must have felt the same vibe because he froze for an instant. She looked up, their eyes met. And then he blinked and walked away to retrieve the knives and spatula they'd used to prepare their meal.

The moment of awareness Becky had felt became a real chill. No matter what secrets and confessions came between them, that physical connection was still there, simmering just beneath the surface.

But knowing Zachariah wasn't as eager to act on that attraction as he'd been eighteen months—hell, even twenty-four hours—ago formed a lump of self-inflicted disappointment in the pit of her stomach. Becky quickly finished loading the dishes and closed the door. Then she wet a dishcloth and began wiping down the kitchen. "I didn't mean to stick you into the middle of all the lies without warning you first. I'll straighten it out with Dad. You don't have to play along."

Zachariah leaned his hips against the edge of the sink, crossing his arms over his chest in a deceptively relaxed pose. He didn't budge when Becky tried to wipe the counter behind him. "How real are these threats against you?"

Becky looked at one bulging forearm, dusted with fine hair that had turned almost golden from the amount of time he'd spent in the sun. She lifted her gaze past the aggressive line of his jaw before meeting the question narrowing his dark green eyes. "You seriously want to do this, don't you?"

"Seriously."

They might be able to talk like civilized people again, but the rawness was still there, leaving her emotions stripped bare and her usual confidence on shaky ground. For the first time, Captain Zachariah Clark, USMC, frightened her almost as much as she suspected he frightened the enemy—whether it was on the battlefield or in her own hometown. This wasn't a man who would do anything halfway—be it making love or keeping her safe.

With a dutiful nod, Becky tossed the cloth into the sink and went out to the antique roll-top desk she kept in the corner of the living room. She knew by his heat and scent that Zachariah was following her again. Pushing up the desk top, she pulled a short stack of papers from one of the cubby holes inside and handed them over. "He left a dead rose on my windshield at work, and one at my front door. I threw those away and erased the phone messages. But I made copies of these. The police have the originals. I copied them because one of the men I forced a settlement from, and am scheduled to meet in court again this week, is an officer with Richmond PD. If he's doing this, I thought it'd be too easy for him to get his hands on the notes and destroy them."

"Nice connections."

"If he's the one. I guess I've pissed off plenty of men in my work. Though Officer Cunningham does have a history of violence against his ex-wife."

The muscles in Zachariah's jaw seemed to tighten as he read each new page. "Is she the client who called yesterday morning?"

Becky nodded. If she approached this discussion the way she did a case, she could keep her emotions in check. "These were hand-delivered to my office and here. There were no postmarks on any of the envelopes."

Zachariah swore as he read the note that promised to take what a man deserved out of her hide if he couldn't get it any other way. "That means he's in the area. Or he has an accomplice who has access to you. Someone he's either duped or who has it in for you, too."

"You're not one for pep talks, are you?"

"This isn't a joke." If that scowl was any indication, she wouldn't be seeing another lopsided grin anytime soon. "What else has this nutcase done?"

If she was going to tell him, she had to tell him everything. Becky opened her bag and pulled out the envelope she'd received that afternoon. "He put this on my car while I was in Dimitra's house today. He was that close to me, and I never saw him." She watched as Zachariah emptied the contents into his hand and studied them. "The watch broke when I dropped the envelope. I don't know what it means other than the reference to time in the note."

"I know what it means. It's a timer." He picked up the coin-shaped disk, and fanned the four wires out, holding them up to see. "Put these together and add some type of explosive and you've got a bomb."

"A bomb?" Becky felt lightheaded. She needed to sit, but she couldn't seem to move. A bomb was more than words. It was more than hate and threats. A bomb meant she wasn't the only one who'd get hurt if he decided to finally make good on his threats.

"Tell me about the calls."

"I've received them here and at work. He hasn't called my cell number."

"Yet."

That made her feel better. *Think, Becky. Don't just react.* "My calls are screened by my assistant at work, so he must have the ability to turn the voice-altering thing on and off. She didn't recognize the voice, and the phone records told the police nothing. Here, I let every call go to the machine first." She pointed to the phone on the end table beside the couch. "Oh, God."

She was reacting.

The red message light was blinking.

She rubbed her hands up and down her arms as the chill tried to reclaim her. "It's probably just Dad, calling to make sure I got home okay. Or a client."

"Yeah, you're huggin' yourself like that because you think it's Daddy callin'."

Zachariah took his warmth across the room and pushed the button. After her recorded message and the requisite beep, a voice that was more annoying than familiar came on. "Becky? Roger Sligh," blared Dimitra Cunningham's former attorney from the answering machine in his bombastic, almost cartoonish voice. "One of these days you're gonna have to answer your own damn phone and talk to me. Your secretary can tell me every story in the book about why you can't meet with me, but you're damn well gonna listen to my side of the case."

"Who is this guy?" Zachariah asked while Roger Sligh ranted on.

"A blowhard with a law degree." Though Roger certainly had reason to carry a grudge against her, she couldn't see him having enough foresight to plan a relentless assault on her sense of security and well-being the way Joe Stalker had done. "My assistant, Cheryl, nicknamed him 'Sligh-me.' Trust me, it fits. He's a cheap attorney who usually represents lowlifes and petty criminals. Dimitra hired him for her initial divorce proceedings. He bungled it so badly I filed a formal complaint with the State Bar against him. It's the fourth case he's botched enough that I've had to step in and clean up his mess."

"Could he lose his license to practice law?"

"If we're lucky."

Zachariah's steely expression dared her to find anything amusing about Roger's call. "Sounds like a good motive for stickin' it to you."

Roger blustered on. "…maybe if I had a rich daddy like you, I could buy my own set of morals, too. Get off your high horse, lady, and retract that complaint. Some of us have to work for a living."

The slam of his phone ended the call.

"That wasn't too bad."

"Any other raving lunatics in your life you want to tell me about?"

"Zachariah…"

But then a second beep sounded. There was a moment of silence and then a sighing sound, like the wind blowing through the leaves of a forest.

Everything in Becky tensed.

"It's him." She knew the sound of his breathing by heart. It crawled across her skin.

There was a brief, soft buzz of static. She braced for the voice that might have sounded like a child's computer game if the words hadn't been so personal.

"Did you get my message? I miss our little chats. I'll be seeing you soon. Tick. Tick. Tick."

Then it was over.

Zachariah swore a pithy blue streak that would have done any Marine proud.

"What you said." Becky had clenched every muscle so tight, it almost hurt to speak. "The coward. That's what I'm dealing with. That's what I'm trying to protect you and my parents from."

"That's why you were so jumpy around Travis. For all you knew, he could be this guy."

"No. I realized right away Travis was a friend of yours. That you trust him." Zachariah breathed deeply, trying to control his anger. Becky had lost count of how many times she'd done the same thing the past few months. "Up till now, it's just been a lot of hot air and mind games. My client is the one who's in real danger. Someone destroyed her garden Saturday night, sabotaged her AC system. I'm sure it was her ex-husband, Nick." She forced the tension from her crossed arms and countered Zachariah's pacing. "If that was him, so help me God—"

"Wait a minute. That's where you went this afternoon? On your own?" The big guy moved amazingly fast when he wanted to get in her face and command her attention. "And you didn't think I needed to know about this?"

"When was I supposed to tell you? Be honest, Zachariah. You're a different man now than you were eighteen months ago. When you got off that bus— when you had that first flashback—I knew you had issues of your own you needed to deal with. You don't need to deal with mine, too."

"I'm tougher than I look." *Impossible.* "I can handle

anything you throw at me. I just need to know everything I'm dealin' with."

"So you expect me to spill my guts to you, but you won't talk about whatever it is you're going through?"

"We're supposed to be on our honeymoon, Beckster. I'm not going to ruin our time together with any of my crap."

"Ditto." She circled the immovable wall and headed for a hot shower and cool pajamas.

"You go on to bed." Zachariah's voice was surprisingly calm and dismissive.

Surprising enough that she turned to face him. "You're not coming?"

"I need some distance if I'm going to come up with a plan of action."

"I said the police are taking care of this."

"And your prime suspect's a cop? I don't think so." He pulled his cell phone off his belt and opened it up to scroll through the numbers. He untied his duffel bag and dumped the contents out on the couch, picking up the holstered pistol that had been buried in the bottom. "I'll need all the details you can give me on this Cunningham case. Whatever's public record. Names. Addresses. Police reports. Anything you can show me. I want the names of anybody else who might have a beef against you, too. You have a computer with Internet access I can use?"

Becky drifted back toward her couch, a little unsure and a lot alarmed about the Marine forming some kind of battle plan in her living room. "I have a laptop in my attaché case. What are you doing?"

"I'm being the bodyguard." He opened her leather bag and dug inside. "I'll call in some friends. If Murphy and Stahlnecker aren't too busy getting laid, they'll help. They're good men from my unit. They can keep an eye on this client of yours, too—find out if it's her ex who's responsible for the damage at her place."

"Wait a minute. This is a woman's life—a family's future we're talking about. Dimitra and her son aren't some game you can play at." She touched his arm, stilling his methodical movements as he set up some kind of command center at her kitchen table.

His muscles flinched beneath her fingertips before he pulled away. He circled the table to find a plug-in for the computer. "Neither is protecting you from the bastard who wrote those notes and collects bomb parts. If I'm going to play the role your daddy assigned to me—"

"You don't have to—"

"—then I'm going to play that part the only way I know how. And that's not to *play* at all. If this guy wants to hurt you, he's SOL. I'm not gonna let it happen."

"That's a little neanderthal of you, isn't it?"

They faced off over the table. "It's who I am, darlin'. You're in danger—I keep you safe."

"The Marine Corps way, huh? Semper Fi and hoo-yah and all that? What if you put my parents or clients in danger by going all gung ho on me like this?" Zachariah suddenly went so still that he seemed to suck all the energy out of the room. *Don't make fun of the Corps.* That felt too much like making fun of the man. And she would never, ever…Becky gripped the chair in front of her. "I'm sorry. That was below the belt. I know the work you do is important to you and vital to our country. I just think you're overreacting. This guy hasn't done anything yet but blow hot air."

"His messages have progressed from a whiny complaint to a specific threat to do you bodily harm. If this was chatter from a terrorist, I'd be armed and ready for an attack."

"He's not a terrorist. We're not at war here."

"*He* is." If Zachariah's expression blanked and he went into one of those fugue states where the nightmare seized control of him, Becky would be well and truly scared of the warrior taking command of her kitchen—and her life.

But his expression remained stern, his eyes clear. "This guy is not going to hurt you. End of discussion." Three steps brought him around the table. He took her by the elbow and walked her to her bedroom door. "You go read a book or soak in the tub or get some sleep. I'll clean up my mess and catch forty winks out here on the couch. I've got work to do."

He turned his back on her and strode back out to the kitchen.

Discussion over.

Apparently, so was the honeymoon.

IT WAS AFTER ONE in the morning when Becky sensed the presence filling her bedroom doorway.

She pushed her hair out of her eyes and sat up, rubbing at the dent in her cheek from where she'd dozed off on top of the file she'd been reviewing. Standing still and silent, he seemed more apparition than man. Even after blinking the sleep from her eyes, Zachariah's face, high above the circle of light cast by the lamp on her bedside table, was wreathed in shadows. But farther down, other than the neat, white boxer shorts he wore, every inch of him, from shoulder to toe, gleamed like a bronzed god in the lamp's circle of soft light.

Definitely a man.

Becky's skin prickled with heat. Her lips and tongue were parched with thirst. She smoothed the tangled neckline of her silk shortie pajamas, catching a strangled gasp in her throat when she accidentally brushed a responsive nipple. She curled her legs beneath her in an instinctively protective gesture as her womb began to throb. It was as though she had awakened to a forbidden lover come to life from her dreams. A familiar lover.

Only, lover-boy wasn't moving any closer. He didn't speak. She couldn't read any gleam in his eye or guess his intentions from his naughty, boyish smile. He just stood there, waiting. Watching.

The subtly erotic morphed into something unsettling. Did his nightmares include sleepwalking? Shaking off her body's ill-timed arousal, Becky scrambled to the edge of the bed and swung her legs over the side. "Zachariah? Are you all right? Say something."

"I don't fit your couch." Gruff. Caustic.

Definitely awake.

"Oh." No nightmare. No danger. No seduction, either. Embarrassment at wanting something he wasn't here to deliver heated her cheeks as much as the relief she felt. Becky gathered her papers and shuffled to the door. "Do you want to switch?"

"No." His arm snaked out and captured her around the waist as she tried to skirt past him. "I want to share."

With no more ceremony than that, he picked her up on his hip and carried her back to the bed. He plucked the folder from her arms and turned off the light before dropping her onto the folded-down sheets and climbing in beside her. Propping himself up on one elbow, he threw his heavy thigh over her legs, pinning her on her back. With his chest pressed to her side, her left arm trapped between them, his hand went straight to the buttons of her shirt, his agile fingers making quick work of opening the front and pushing the material to either side. Exposed to the air-conditioned atmosphere, her nipples tightened and pearled. But the chill didn't last. His palm was soon there, covering one breast and then the other, smoothing away the goose bumps on the surface, kindling a different kind of warmth from the inside out.

"I hate fighting with you." He splayed his hand across her belly and leaned over her to kiss the swell of her breast, to wet the tip with his tongue. He rubbed his sandpapery jaw over the straining bead and she bucked at the sharp bolt of electricity that shot straight down between her thighs. Her free hand came up to his shoulder, giving a token push against too much, too fast. The crisp curl of his chest hair abraded the nipple yet again as he raised his head to capture her tortured cry with his lips.

With a sighing surrender, her world falling into

place once more, Becky welcomed him into her mouth
and curled her fingertips into the corded muscle of his
tricep, trying to pull him closer.

As his weight and warmth pressed into her body, his
hand slipped beneath the elastic waist of her silk shorts
to cup her center. His lips and tongue performed a leisurely, thorough exploration of her mouth, but his hand
was on a different, more urgent mission.

Pushing down against her with the heel of his palm,
he stroked his fingers along her lips, once, twice, then
thrust them inside her. Pinned beneath the restricting
bands of his thigh and body, Becky writhed helplessly
as he massaged her deep inside, slicking his fingers
with her essence, pulling out to tangle them in her
thatch of golden hair and tease the inside of her thighs
before thrusting them in again.

She tried to lift her hips to meet him halfway, but
all she could do was slide her hand up to his neck and
hold on as her pulse raced and her breathing grew
shallow. Like flint and steel striking together, an ember
was lit and Becky could only wait and wonder as the
blaze spread and consumed her. He caught her nub
between her pelvic bone and his hand, building the
pressure from both inside and out—until she climaxed,
and tiny spasms of muscle danced around his fingers
like sparks popping from a fire.

Becky whimpered into his mouth, at once replete
yet yearning for more. Only then did he lift his head.
Even in the dim illumination from the moon and street-
light outside her window, she could see a matching
heat still smoldering in his deep green eyes. He pulled

his hand from her pants and rested it on the rise and fall of her stomach as her breathing began to even out. Her own musky scent tinted the air with sex and intimacy and a mutual need that frightened her with its power yet humbled her right down to the core.

He'd had his way with her and she'd loved every minute of it. But it wasn't enough. With Zachariah, she wanted something more. Something that an orgasm alone could never satisfy.

And then she felt the rock-hard evidence of all he was holding back push against her hip. Right next to her trapped hand. Her fingertips brushed against the moist cotton of his shorts where the first drops of his desire had soaked through.

A slow smile blossomed on her lips.

Not so helpless, after all.

Maneuvering the only way she could, Becky wrapped her fingers around him and squeezed. Zachariah lurched in her hand. "Easy," he warned. He brushed away a hair that had caught in the corner of her mouth and bent down to place a gentle kiss there. "Am I forgiven for being a bullheaded SOB?"

She touched his handsome mouth and caressed his scruffy jaw, frowning at the gravelly sound of apology in his tone. "There's nothing to forgive. Just a lot left to learn about each other. I'm sorry I kept so many secrets."

He turned his lips into her palm and kissed the tender flesh there. "Logically, I understand why you did it. You thought you were doing what was best for your family."

Something small and tight, cold and lonely inside

her—that had nothing to do with sex and everything to do with a deeper, emotional connection—began to unfurl like a tiny bud, ready to bloom under Zachariah's honest, tender attention.

"I hate fighting, too. Loving is ever so much better."

He grinned. "At your command."

There were no more words. In a flurry of hands and needs, his shorts and her pajamas quickly disappeared. After sparing a moment to sheathe himself, Zachariah angled her across the bed, stretched her arms above her head and guided her hands to the bedpost. Becky held on as Zachariah nudged her thighs open and covered her body with his.

The bed rocked, the new mattress held. Zachariah lifted Becky up to that plateau of pleasure only he could create before they tumbled over the precipice together and landed safely in each other's arms.

Some time later, when Becky could catch her breath and think clearly again, she cuddled up against Zachariah in the middle of the bed. Lying skin to skin, their legs entwined, she needed no other pillow than his shoulder, no other cover but the warmth of his body wrapped around hers.

While she breathed in the salty fragrance of maleness and perspiration off his skin, she traced absent lines up and down the length of his throat. "Question."

"Yeah?"

She savored the drowsy vibration of sound beneath her fingertips. "What if this turns out to be the only way you and I can communicate with each other?

What if the bedroom is the only place where you and I get along?"

He captured her roving hand and pulled it down to his chest, holding it over the strong beat of his heart. "I've been wondering that myself."

With a wistful resignation, she followed up with another question. "We can't base a lifelong commitment on the lust we feel. What if it burns out and there's nothing else there?"

"I know." Curling his arm behind her back, he brushed a tendril of hair off her cheek and tucked it behind her ear. "I've been doing some strategizing about us."

"You've been thinking about this?"

"Yes. I've been lookin' at this from different angles, and I think this is something we should try." She waited expectantly to hear his battle strategy. "We need to shift our relationship into Reverse. We've already had the wedding, and we don't seem to have any problem consummating it. What if we do something radical— like go on a date?"

She smiled against his skin. "You mean, pretend like we've just met and we're getting to know each other?"

"We don't have to pretend. We don't know each other all that well when you think about it. You've never been skinny-dipping. I've never been to an A-list political gala."

"You'll hate it."

"More than you know. But I look pretty sharp in my dress blues. Unless you prefer me in a tuxedo like your dad said?"

Becky was already salivating over mental images of Zachariah in his dress uniform with a sword and white hat versus a coal-black tux, tailored to fit those shoulders. "I suppose it's not helpful if I say I prefer you in your birthday suit?"

He laughed. "See? I've learned something already. If I were to take you to lunch, where would we go?"

"Italian food. I'm a sucker for pasta—almost any kind. Though the size of my hips forces me to limit how often I indulge myself."

His hand slid from her back to her butt and squeezed. "Your hips are gorgeous."

"But you're a boob man, right?"

"I think I'm more of a Beckster man. It's the package, not the parts."

It was her turn to laugh. "Are there fish and slimy things in that lake of yours?"

"Oh, yeah. The fish like to nip at you, but they don't really bite. It's more like little kisses." When she cringed, he gave her rump a gentle swat. "You'll pick a stranger up in a bar and marry him, but you won't take a dive into a lake?"

"Not if there's *slimy* involved. I'll have to work up to that one."

"We won't try everything all at once?" He kissed the crown of her hair and settled back more comfortably onto the pillows. "Oh, and we're moving this show to your parents' house. From what I could see, the security system on their estate is a hell of a lot more modern and reliable than the setup here at your apartment complex. I only have a few weeks to ID this guy, and I want you someplace safe while I'm doin' it."

A few weeks. Then he'd be gone. Would their relationship withstand another lengthy separation? Would it even survive this short time they had together?

Ignoring her own fatigue, Becky pushed herself up beside him. "Stay at Mom and Dad's? We won't have much privacy. And since they think we're not married, they won't let us stay in the same room."

"Even better." He kissed away her pout of protest. "That will make it that much harder for us to fall into bed together—not that I'm against that idea—but I don't want to give in to the easy fix if we have another disagreement."

"You think we will?"

"Independent woman? Hardheaded Marine? I know we will. We'll have to actually talk things out, find other ways to get close."

She settled back down beside him. "I like a challenge."

"I want us to work. Not just for a few nights. But forever."

"Me, too." There was a long, long pause. Their breathing synchronized and slowed, but a terrible, nagging thought kept Becky from falling asleep. Finally, she had to ask. "What if we don't work out, big guy? What if Joe Stalker or my parents—or us—keep that from happening?"

Troubling thoughts must have kept Zachariah awake, as well. "I'll take care of Joe. You take care of your parents."

"Who takes care of you and me not screwing us up?"

The fingers drawing circles at the small of her back was the only sign that he was still listening. But he had no answer for her.

"Good night, Beckster."

8

"IF I HAD KNOWN I WAS reporting for duty this morning,
I'd have had Deke cut me off a few beers sooner last
night. Those Southern girls sure know how to party."
Thomas Murphy had provided almost all of the conversation since meeting Becky and Zachariah outside
her office building at a quarter to nine that morning.
With black hair, blue eyes and a gift for gab,
Zachariah's friend fit his Irish roots down to a tee. A
lanky package of perpetual motion, he shifted back
and forth on the balls of his feet, watching the
numbers light up as the elevator carried them to the
twelfth floor. "How much are we gettin' paid for this
gig, anyway?"

A flick of a glance from Zachariah seemed to give
him his answer.

"Oh. It's one of those volunteer details, eh?"

With Zachariah standing between them, Becky
couldn't see the unspoken message that passed from
Captain to Lieutenant. But from Murphy's wiseacre
tone, she got the feeling he was a man who liked to
push the limits of decorum and authority, almost as
much as the Zachariah she was getting to know liked

to keep things—and people—in a tidy, predictable order. Thomas Murphy would drive her father crazy.

Becky liked him immediately.

She leaned forward on the toes of her taupe Ferragamo pumps to speak to Murphy. "How much would you *like* to be paid for your services, Lieutenant?"

Now that green-eyed glance slanted her way and Zachariah growled, "He could have said no."

Becky wondered at the bond of respect and brotherhood that would prompt Murphy and a stockier man, Lieutenant Deke Stahlnecker, to give up their leave time to grant Zachariah's request for assistance. Maybe if she studied Murphy long enough, she'd begin to understand something about how military men interacted with each other. Stahlnecker, a Richmond native who'd uttered little more than a courteous "Pleased to meet you, ma'am" didn't give her the same chance to get acquainted. At Zachariah's direction, he'd jotted down Dimitra Cunningham's address and driven away.

"Right. Like he's going to turn down an order from a superior officer. I know that much about military life. Besides, you've got your grouchy face on, and nobody wants to say no to that."

Murphy laughed. "I like you already, Mrs. Clark. You can start by calling me Thomas. Or Murphy. But not Lieutenant. Not while I'm on home soil."

"Mrs. Clark?" The name sounded strange to Becky's ears, but it had rolled right off Murphy's tongue as though it was the right thing to call her. Well, technically, it *was* the right thing to call her. But no one had. And no one would now that, for her parents' sake, she and Zachariah were pretending they weren't married at all. "Maybe you'd better just call me Becky."

"Will do, ma'am." Murphy didn't seem to recognize an awkward moment, or else he was polite enough to let it pass. "Say, you got any coffee in this place?"

"My assistant, Cheryl, brews a mean pot every morning. Or if you prefer something fancy like a latte, there's a coffee shop about a block down the street to the west."

"Murphy will drink whatever your assistant has prepared." Becky rolled her eyes as Zachariah's pronouncement came down from above. "I need him to take a look at your computer and phone setup. Plus, I can use an extra pair of eyes around your office."

Becky tilted her chin. "You understand there are files in my office you can't have access to, right? Attorney-client privilege? State business? And you can't interfere with the office routine. There are other attorneys and their staff who share the suite with me. Some of them may have clients coming in." She poked her finger against the sleeve of the tan suit coat he wore. "So don't walk in there with your big shoulders and your combat face, looming up behind innocent people and scaring the crap out of them, okay?"

The temperature in the elevator rose in direct proportion to the narrowing squint of Zachariah's eyes. There was no answering "okay," no deal struck. Murphy loosed a low whistle between his teeth, feeling the fallout from the battle of wills.

"Murphy…" Zachariah warned, never taking his eyes off Becky.

The number twelve lit up as the elevator dinged. "Saved by the bell. I'll let you two work this out." Murphy darted out before the doors had fully opened.

Shaking her head at the mule-headed Marine beside her, Becky moved forward to follow Murphy.

But Zachariah grabbed her arm and pulled her back inside as he punched the door-close button with his other hand. For one second she thought he meant to steal a kiss. But when she turned to face him, it wasn't passion that blazed in his eyes. "Remember. I'm the bodyguard, not your husband, now. If I say run, you run. If I say duck, you dive for cover. Otherwise, I'll try to stay in the background as much as I can to get some research done on those names you gave me."

"I know you don't mean to make things difficult, but—"

"Now's not the time for an attitude, darlin'. You've got to take this guy seriously." He hunched down as though bringing that humorless scowl to her level would drive the point home. "You don't go anywhere without me. You don't open your mail on your own. You don't answer the phone unless I'm there to listen in. Got that?"

Becky drew on all the ice of her Norwegian roots to keep her temper out of her voice. Understanding that he was motivated by a need to protect her helped. Understanding why the fun-loving man she'd impulsively married had to go away in order to do this job…? Well, there was no understanding this harder, more driven version of her husband. Instead of losing her cool, however, she straightened the knot of his tie and patted the summer-weight wool of his lapel. "Do you see bars on my collar or stripes on my sleeve? Watching my back is fine—ordering me around like one of your men is not. Got *that?*"

She turned away and opened the door.

BECKY FINISHED THE MONDAY morning staff meeting with the first tendrils of a headache spiking through her temples. After fielding a barrage of questions about the leviathan in the suit and tie and unsmiling face lurking around the office, she was more ready than ever to get down to work on anything that remotely resembled a legal case, instead of feeling as if she'd been put on the witness stand herself to be picked apart by well-meaning coworkers.

Yes, at her father's insistence, she'd hired a security consultant. Why? Because she'd received some threats. No, they didn't seem to be targeted at the public advocates' office, but specifically to her. Yes, he and his assistant might be asking other attorneys and staff for information, but no, he didn't think anyone else was in any sort of danger and they'd be as conscientious as possible about not upsetting anyone's routine. In addition to the building guards and checkpoints the State already provided, Mr. Clark and his men would be upgrading security measures to ensure that everyone on the entire floor was kept safe.

Her assistant, Cheryl, continued the inquisition— after the meeting had ended and she'd brought two ibuprofen and a stack of phone messages into Becky's office. Her coppery curls bounced around her face as she peeked out the door into her adjacent office to make sure Zachariah and Murphy were still engrossed with the computer files they'd been reading.

The younger woman bopped over to Becky's desk and ducked closer with a conspiratorial whisper. "Those two are hot, aren't they? I didn't see a ring on either of them. You don't think they're married, do you? I mean, men like that don't get married, right?" Becky opened her mouth to comment, but Cheryl saved her the trouble of telling a lie by rushing on to her next thought. "This isn't like that movie, is it? You aren't sleeping with one of the bodyguards, are you? I mean who wouldn't want to? Especially that Mr. Murphy with the blue eyes. Yum."

Feigning a bit of shock at the idea of her going to bed with a man she'd just met, Becky picked up the stack of messages and turned her back on the open doorway and the "hot" bodyguard she was, indeed, sleeping with.

"Focus, Cheryl."

"Oh, come on." Cheryl scooted around to Becky's side of the desk. "You mean to tell me it doesn't give you a little bit of a thrill to have those two paying such close attention to you? That big guy has that whole scary enforcer thing going for him, like he's with the mob or something. But that Thomas Murphy…" *Oh, my. Did Cheryl just lick her lips?* "He said my hair reminded him of his lucky penny. Do you think he meant anything by lucky?"

"I don't know either one of them very well." The fact that her words were truer than she'd like them to be pinged at her headache. Dismissing the discomfiting thought as well as her assistant's eager speculation, Becky dropped the messages onto her desk and reached for her coffee mug to swallow the pills. "Plus, I have work to do, so I don't have time to be thrilled. If George Wesley or my father calls—or someone related to the Barclay fund-raiser—put them straight through. Otherwise, take a message. I need to get caught up on my paperwork. I'd also like you to get those notes typed up for the Cunningham hearing tomorrow."

"Okay." Cheryl's disappointment that the conversation had ended was palpable. "I guess those phone calls do have you spooked if you can see Mr. Murphy and Mr. Clark as only the hired help. Do I need to be worried?"

Perhaps her tongue had been too sharp and her nerves too frazzled to remember that Cheryl was her friend, that they had shot the breeze before over the plusses and negatives of eligible men who came into the office. If Becky wasn't behaving enough like herself that her closest friends questioned her, then maybe Joe Stalker's messages were affecting her more than she realized. And she refused to let him have that much power over her.

"I'm sorry. It's the headache. And no, I don't think this kook is any threat to you or anyone else." Becky forced herself to smile. "And, Cheryl?" Her assistant's hazel eyes widened expectantly, no doubt bracing for another impersonal word. "Mr. Murphy will be working at the spare table in your office today. Try not to drool on your desk."

Cheryl giggled as the tension diffused. "No guar-

antees on that one. I'll bring in those notes as soon as
I get them typed up."

"Thanks." Becky sat and rolled her chair over to her
desk.

But her smile didn't last beyond the closing of her
door. Mostly because her door didn't close. A big
shoulder, easily recognizable, even in a slicked-up city
suit, nudged its way inside. Zachariah carried in a thicker
than normal attaché case. Without so much as a "Hello"
or "Excuse me" or "Mind if I come in?" he paused,
scanned three-hundred-and-sixty degrees around the
shelves and file cabinets and spotted his target. Then he
crossed the room in three long strides and proceeded to
clear her potted plants and law school award off the
bookshelf behind her desk. He opened the case, which
wasn't an attaché at all but rather some kind of portable
communication setup, complete with dials and headphones and a telephone receiver. He plugged something
in, extended an antenna and then squatted beside her
chair to pull a bundle of cords from underneath her desk.

When he pulled out a pocketknife and sliced
through the plastic ring binding the cords together,
Becky decided one of them needed to speak. "I'm not
in your way, am I?"

There was barely a flicker of an eyebrow as he continued to work. "Like I promised, Murph and I are
staying in the background."

"You're six-and-a-half-feet tall, Zachariah. There's
no *background* for you." She swiveled her chair toward
Cheryl's office and pointed. "And Murphy's blue eyes
have already disrupted the routine around here."

"Murphy can get more information in one day by winkin' those pretty blues than a platoon of interrogators can get in a week. What little he can't accomplish with a computer, that sweet-talkin' Irish bull of his can. Once Deke reports in with his reconnaissance of the Cunningham place and a couple of demolition suppliers in the area, Murphy will feed the information into the profile he's creating. He's my best shot at narrowing the list of Becky Owens fans without involving the police."

High-tech equipment. Reconnaissance. Interrogations. A nervous suspicion twisted in the pit of Becky's stomach. "What exactly is it you and your friends do for the Marines?"

"Detection, intervention and suppression of hostile targets. We also provide ancillary support for air and ground units as needed."

Military gobbledygook. "Which means?"

"Which means I can't tell you about my job."

Which meant getting to know this man—getting closer to him in other areas besides the bedroom—was growing more difficult by the minute. The more time she spent with him, the more she realized she'd married a stranger. For instance, she'd known Zachariah was good with his hands, but the speedy efficiency with which he stripped the plastic off two different wires and clipped on an attachment from the box before taping them off and placing them back beneath her desk made her wonder what else he'd used those hands for besides rigging equipment and making love.

"Where did you get all this gear?"

"Travis McCormick."

"Your friend at Quantico who's going to train special Marines to do…whatever it is you do?"

He nodded. "I explained the situation and he offered to help in any way he could. As of ten-hundred hours this morning, Murphy, Deke and I are conducting an unofficial test run to make sure all this equipment is in working order."

Becky watched him go back to the box and flip a switch. He put the headphones to one ear and adjusted a dial. "None of this is illegal, is it?" she asked.

"I'm a man of honor, darlin'. Excuse me, Miss Owens." He turned off the machine and put down the headphones. "This isn't some top-secret prototype. All this does is allow me to listen in on your phone, and record it if it turns out to be our friend so we can analyze the equipment he's using and possibly deconstruct the message to get a voice print and identify him."

"That's all?"

He understood the sarcasm, but he didn't laugh. "I told you I'm not playing at this. I intend to stop this bastard *before* he can hurt you."

Zachariah towered above her. Becky tilted her head back, searching for some sign of his boyish smile or the tender hunger that had blazed in his eyes last night. But the look reflected in his unblinking green gaze was far closer to the distant desolation of his flashbacks and nightmares than to the sexual adventurer who'd swept her off her feet at Groucho's Pub so many months ago.

She'd traded her lover for a protector. And the jury was still out on whether or not she'd made a smart deal. What if this get-acquainted-outside-the-bedroom plan failed, and they couldn't find any other way to connect? They came from different backgrounds, shared little in common. She refused to bend and he was inflexible. How did they build a long-term relationship on that shaky foundation? What if they couldn't? What if she'd already lost him?

The possibility hit her like a blow to the gut.

Becky lowered her gaze and spun in her chair to stare sightlessly at the words on her computer screen. Losing Zachariah. *That* thought scared her more than a robotic message on her answering machine.

The telephone at her elbow rang, jangling into her thoughts, and Becky jumped as though the mechanical voice had already shouted something vile into her ear. "Damn! I hate that thing."

She pressed a palm over her pounding heart and snatched the receiver.

Suddenly, Zachariah's hand was there, covering hers. "Easy."

For a moment, she recalled his gentleness, his utter care to always make things right for her. The phone rang again, but she barely heard it. Savoring Zachariah's warmth, needing it more than she cared to admit, Becky breathed out her tension and nodded her thanks.

But his touch had been about business, not comfort. As soon as he saw she was thinking and not just reacting, he pulled away. He turned on his listening machine, put the headphones over his ears, then pointed to her to pick up the call.

Hiding her disappointment—in herself for caring too much about his intentions—she answered the phone. "Becky Owens."

"George Wesley here."

"George." A real live human being. Someone who actually wanted to have an honest conversation with her. "Good morning. You're getting back to me a lot sooner than I expected. What did you find out about Nick Cunningham?"

Becky angled her chair away from Zachariah so she couldn't see the focused intensity that transformed his expression as they discussed their prime suspect for Joe Stalker.

"I've got bad news and worse," the chief of police continued. "First, that tan SUV you asked about doesn't belong to him. Cunningham drives a pickup."

"I knew that. I thought he might have purchased a second vehicle, or borrowed it. Can he account for his whereabouts Saturday night?"

She already knew the answer in her gut, but let the chief speak so that Zachariah could hear it, too. "He claims he was asleep at his apartment. Alone. Not much of an alibi, but then there's no evidence to put him at the scene of the crime, either. I did tell his TAC supervisor to restrict him to desk duty, pending further investigation of the incident."

"TAC? The Tactical Assistance Command unit?" As in bomb squad? Weapons disposal? Hostage standoffs? She glanced up at Zachariah. She could tell by the tic in his jaw that he recognized the term, too. "Are you kidding? Last I knew, Cunningham was a plainclothes officer. How did he get into a tactical unit?"

Chief Wesley's sigh sounded equally as disgusted. "He put in for the move about six months ago. He took the classes. Passed the test. Proved competency in each of the skills and was granted the transfer."

"Don't you have to pass a psych exam to get an assignment like that?"

"He passed with flying colors. His division psychologist said he completed the anger management course and has kept all his scheduled follow-up appointments. He's even joined AA."

Was it possible for a violent man like Nick Cunningham to truly reform himself? Dimitra Cunningham didn't believe it. And up until now, Becky hadn't even considered it a possibility. But Nick had already proved himself one hell of an actor. For years, he had punished and controlled his wife without giving any hint of his brutality to the outside world.

Not until Dimitra had found the courage to stand up and testify against him. Not until she had Becky standing with her to make that testimony stick.

If Nick Cunningham was a good enough actor to convince a judge that *he* made a better parent for his son in the initial divorce proceedings, then he might be a good enough actor to convince a police psychologist that he was a changed man now. One who could be trusted to help, not hurt. Not threaten to make Becky pay for humiliating his male pride.

"So you don't think Nick Cunningham is capable of trashing his ex's most prized possessions to scare her away from speaking out against him in court? If the judge rules in our favor, he'll owe her thousands of dollars in back alimony and child support."

"I can't say what I don't know." Becky heard another voice across the line from George's office, and knew he had to end the call. "Despite Cunningham's history, there hasn't been a single complaint filed against him in two years. Not until your report this weekend. Without concrete evidence to arrest him, my hands are tied. I have to give him the benefit of the doubt."

"I understand, George. Thank you for your help."

"I'll see you at the party on Saturday. I hope everything has smoothed over for your client by then."

"Me, too. Goodbye."

Becky hung up the phone and looked to Zachariah. "Well? I was so sure Nick was the man harassing me. Should I be giving him the benefit of the doubt, too?"

Zachariah hooked the headphones over the top of his machine and propped his hip on the corner of her desk. "If Cunningham's a TAC officer, he'd have access to the technology used to distort a phone message. He'd have access and the know-how to use a variety of weapons and explosives and psychological tactics, as well."

"Sounds like the perfect profile for Joe Stalker." Becky shook her head. She hated when she had a puzzle to solve, but couldn't make the pieces fall into place. "If George Wesley is right, though, Nick may not have been the one to hurt Dimitra this time. And if he's not trying to intimidate her, then why bother coming after me?"

"Just because a man is innocent of one crime doesn't mean he's not guilty of another."

Becky turned her chair away from the cynical words of wisdom. "You really need to work on your pep talks."

Zachariah caught the arm of her chair and swung her back to face him. He leaned in, reached out…and clasped the back of her chair just above her shoulder. So close and yet so far away from the comforting touch she craved. "I just want you to be smart. And safe. I'm not ready to eliminate any possibilities yet. You shouldn't be, either."

"I'm not." She stared hard at the center of his chest, avoiding another glimpse of the distant, detached expression he invariably wore in his bodyguard role. "But I wish you weren't doing as good a job of scaring me as *he* does."

And just when she thought she might never see the warmer, more intimate side of Zachariah again, he stroked the side of her neck. Her breath caught and her eyes drifted shut as she savored the welcome contact. He cupped her face and, with gentle fingertips, massaged circles at her temple. For a blessed moment, the bodyguard disappeared and the man returned. "Headache?"

Becky turned her cheek into his palm, purring in her throat like a cat being petted. "Stress, I'm sure."

His caress calmed her, centered her, tapped into something deeper than the need to be touched.

"I lost somebody." His voice was so low, less than a whisper. Becky held her breath and listened. "A man in my unit. I've lost men before but…" His fingers fluttered against her skin, then stopped moving altogether. "This was my fault. I tried to save him."

Becky covered his hand, held it against her cheek and waited for him to tell more.

"I know I'm bein' a hard-ass about this." His chest expanded before her eyes with a deep, shaky breath. "But I *need* you to be safe."

Ignoring the roles they were playing, Becky pushed to her feet and moved closer. The outside of her thigh brushed against his. Her breast nudged his arm. She reached up to touch his face, to comfort him, to reassure him. To keep him talking about this nightmare buried in his soul. "Zachariah, I—"

He heard the intrusion before she did, stood and walked away.

"Becky, there's a James Enderle…oops." Cheryl stepped in the doorway. "Sorry."

Cheryl probably had missed Zachariah's hasty escape, but Becky was a beat slower to put a mask back on and remember how to smile. She wished she could turn her back on the tender moment and pretend it had never happened. Zachariah already had. "What about James?"

"He's on line one. Says he's an old family friend. I didn't know if you wanted me to put him through."

Becky nodded. "It'll be about the reception Saturday. I'll talk to him."

Zachariah was busy with his gadgets and dials again when Cheryl pointed to him and mouthed the question to Becky, "You okay?"

No. She was weary of being afraid, lonesome for the man behind her and anxious to pursue his revelation. She was guessing that was the key to his nightmares. For an instant, his face had transformed into an expression of such torment that she'd wanted to weep. With him. For him. But as he'd informed her last night, he wasn't really interested in discussing any of his *crap* with her.

Instead, Becky smiled so Cheryl wouldn't worry. She carried on with the task at hand. It was the Owens way. "Line one?"

Cheryl nodded and closed the door behind her. Becky turned to Zachariah. He already had the headset on. "Ready?"

Of course, he was. He was a Marine—right down to the bone. He was a man of action, used to giving orders and expecting them to be followed, used to taking them and doing the same. He fought hard, loved hard and hated mixing the two. He could turn his emotions on and off—he could even deny the demons inside him if that's what it took to get the job done.

Maybe she and Zachariah had something else in common, after all.

Why wasn't *that* discovery such a comforting thought?

Smoothing her skirt beneath her, Becky sat and picked up the phone. "James? Becky here. What can I do for you?"

9

ZACHARIAH SAT TWO TABLES away from Becky at the Generals of the Old South restaurant, polishing off his lunch with a dish of apple-peach cobbler that, in his opinion, did a lot more to earn the restaurant its four-star reputation than the fancy white tablecloths and historic reproduction china that was a little too delicate for his big hands.

Seated so that she remained in his line of sight and wearing an earpiece to hear her conversation—in case she spotted one of the Joe Stalker possibilities on the list Murphy had put together—Zachariah began to speculate on Becky's comment yesterday that blending into the background wasn't much of an option for him. In the Corps, on a mission, being a big bad boy with an eye for trouble and the ability to neutralize that trouble in any number of ways was an advantage. But here in the civilian world, *big* and *bad* made him stand out in a crowd like this one, where the political movers and shakers of Richmond's Capitol Hill area stole glances at him as though *he* were the trouble they needed to keep an eye on.

He didn't begrudge Becky her social standing—

nah, she made the conservative suits she wore for work look sexy, and her sharp-eyed confidence beneath the guise of her cultured, ladylike exterior was one of the things he admired about her. Not to mention how hot it was to know that the coolest, toughest lady in the room had a secret passionate alter ego.

But the differences between them in a setting like this one seemed to push them even farther apart than their eighteen-month separation had. He was the hired help, the odd man out in her day-to-day world. She was right at home with her after-meal coffee and fine china, chatting up party plans with her old family friend, James Enderle.

James Enderle with an engineering degree from M.I.T. and a masters in political science from George-town. James Enderle with the golden hair and pricey suit and manicured nails. James Enderle who was neither *old,* nor—if the number of times he found a way to touch Becky was any indication—interested in being just a friend.

This James Enderle was hittin' on his woman. But because of the role Zachariah had volunteered to play—the bodyguard, not the husband—he couldn't do a damn thing about it.

It was more important that he concentrate on the job at hand. He had to nail the bastard who wanted to hurt Becky before his leave was up. And he didn't even want to consider what might happen if six weeks wasn't long enough. No way could he go back to a war zone with his head on straight if he failed to ensure her safety here at home.

So Zachariah had to sit here and listen and watch as the young Republican clone dropped names of D.C. power brokers and community leaders between stroking the back of Becky's hand and asking if she remembered the time when they were in middle school and they'd baked cookies in the kitchen with his family's housekeeper, Alberta. Apparently, Becky had gotten some of the cookie dough in her hair and James had taken the opportunity to put his hands on her then, too, to help clean her up. He was touching her hair now, reaching across the table, commenting on the cut and how sleek and sophisticated it looked compared to the teenaged girl with doughy curls.

Zachariah returned his coffee cup to its saucer before he crushed it in his fist. *Green* was not a good color on him. Setting aside the wide possessive streak he'd just discovered, Zachariah forced himself to scan the staff and patrons of the bustling restaurant one more time to see if anyone was paying more attention to Becky than he should be.

Besides the handsy Mr. Enderle.

Becky's refined laugh in his earpiece wasn't its normally soothing tonic to Zachariah, but it did draw his attention back to her table. She shook her hair free from Enderle's fingers and sat back beyond arm's reach.

Bravo, darlin'.

"I promise we'll do more than serve cookies for Senator Barclay," Becky said. "The caterer is going with a buffet-style service with hors d'oeuvre versions of appetizers, entrées, salads and desserts. That will make the seating arrangements more open and relaxed, more conducive to conversation than setting up formal tables and serving courses, I think."

"I like it," Enderle agreed, sitting back in his chair after being denied the opportunity to grope. "Down-home Southern hospitality with a cosmopolitan flair."

"I hope the senator will be pleased."

But Golden Boy wasn't giving up on the flirtation. "I should have known the party was in good hands when Bertram informed me you were taking over the arrangements. Our guests with deep pockets won't be able to resist the hostess with the prettiest blue eyes in all of Virginia."

Back off, buddy. Those blue eyes are mine.

"I know Ralph Barclay and Mom go back a long way. She's been a supporter of his since he first ran for State office." Becky was too smart to miss the personal connections Enderle kept trying to make, but, thank goodness, she was ignoring his overtures. Even after only a few days of watching and learning about her, it was clear to Zachariah that when the woman got down to business, she focused on business. James, who'd known Becky for at least fifteen years or so, had yet to clue in on that fact.

"Ralph appreciates that. I hope this late change in plans doesn't mean Lily's taken a turn for the worse. She's been a vital part of Richmond politics for so many years. I know worrying about her has been a burden on you." So ol' James was trying a different tactic to keep things personal.

Something about Becky's smile tightened as Enderle found a chink in her armor. Zachariah had yet

to meet Lily Owens—they'd gotten to the house so late
the night before that she'd already retired to bed. But
there was no doubt about the love Becky had for her
parents, no doubt that she'd do anything—double her
workload, move back home, even hide a marriage—to
protect them.

Zachariah sat forward, watching the uncharacteristic hesitation to Becky's response. *Jackass.* If Enderle
stepped over the line in any way…

But Becky was a trooper. She sucked up whatever
sadness had briefly gotten to her and continued as
though there was no reason for concern. "Mom is
holding her own. But the recovery drains a lot of her
energy. She's still looking forward to attending. I'm
just helping out so she can rest up this week. I'm sure
she'd love it if you asked her for a dance. I think she's
worried about being reduced to a wallflower. You know
how she loves to chat up her favorite causes."

"Tell her I'm counting on her. And she'll be the first
name on my dance card." Enderle motioned for their
server to bring them some more coffee and used the
gesture to stretch his arm across the table and silently
ask for her hand. "After you, of course."

Zachariah zoomed in on that pretty boy's hand and
waited for Becky to show him she was too smart to
take the bait. But there must be something about polite
society or pretending to be single he didn't understand. Because she smiled—smiled!—and placed her
hand in his.

Enderle's butt was saved by the vibrating hum of the
phone on Zachariah's belt. And the ever so slight, but

important distinction in Becky's response. "*She'll* look forward to it."

Yeah, Golden Boy, you dance with Mama and I will escort Becky to the dance floor. Of course, in reality, that wasn't gonna happen. After a late-night discussion with Bertram Owens regarding coordinating Zachariah's security team with the senator's contingent on Saturday, it was clear that Zachariah wasn't going to get the chance to dance with his own wife. He'd be working, not mingling with the guests. He'd be relegated to the background, which was such a lousy fit for him.

His phone buzzed again. He pulled it off his belt and opened it. "What?"

"It's Deke, sir."

Even though he'd recognized the number, he'd snapped at his friend all the same. "Sorry. This hoity-toity lunch is startin' to wear on my nerves a little. What's up?"

"I've got the information you wanted on bomb parts in the area." Deke swallowed a curse at something—maybe he'd dropped his notepad—before reporting. "One construction company, Matalin—they're a pretty big deal here in Richmond—has some missing inventory of demolition supplies. Wires, triggers, blasting caps, C-4."

"Would Cunningham or anyone else on that list have access to Matalin's stuff?"

"His TAC team did a sweep of the construction site where the equipment went missing, but that was after the theft had already been reported."

"He could have stolen the goods, then used the TAC sweep to cover his tracks."

Deke's breath hissed in a tight, controlled sound before responding. "Possibly. There's another distant connection, a Rocky Alvarez who worked in demo before the Matalin foreman fired him."

Zachariah scrolled through the memorized list of suspects in his head. "I don't remember Becky prosecuting anyone named Alvarez."

"No, but Alvarez is a two-bit punk with a history of petty crimes. The attorney who's represented him more than once is Roger Sligh."

Ding. They had a hit on their list. "Becky's assistant calls him 'Sligh-me.' Becky filed a complaint against him with the State Bar for gross incompetence."

"Getting disbarred would be reason enough to have a grudge against her."

Zachariah nodded, glad to see Becky pulling her hand back into her lap. He switched his focus away from Deke long enough to hear Enderle discussing the senator's appearance at the reception again. "I want to create a little drama."

He'd give Golden Boy some drama if he didn't do a better job of keeping his hands to himself on Saturday night.

"You still there, Captain?" Deke's tightlipped grunt drew Zachariah's attention back to the phone call.

"Sligh could be the so-called brains of the operation, terrorizing Becky and throwing suspicion onto Cunningham, while Alvarez or some other lowlife he's defended puts together a bomb for him."

"Of course, if it is Cunningham behind this, he'd have access to bomb equipment through the police department." Another grunt ended Deke's sentence.

"You okay?" Zachariah glanced away from Becky and Enderle. Deke Stahlnecker had never been one to complain, even when he had been carrying a piece of shrapnel in his leg and was slowly bleeding toward unconsciousness. All the more reason to check on his man. "You have a run-in with Cunningham when you were checking out the house?"

"No. But we may have a situation with *Mrs.* Cunningham."

"Explain."

"She came home to get a backpack for her kid at school while I was snooping around the place."

"Did she see you?"

"I got out of the house, but I ran into her coming down the front steps. I think she thought I was a cop—accused me of working with her ex and that I was there planting evidence or something like that. I couldn't understand everything she was saying." There was another hiss of breath. "She was backing away from me the whole time—sometimes talking English, sometimes some Russian language."

"You show her your ID? Mention you were helpin' Becky?"

"She wasn't in the mood to listen. She kept cowering away like she thought I was about to smack her. I've never hit a woman in my life, Captain. I swear."

"That's Cunningham's legacy. I'm not gonna let him do the same to Becky." Zachariah heard the distant sound of classical music, and realized he was hearing Becky's phone ringing through his ear piece. She excused herself from Enderle and bent down to pull her phone from her purse. Zachariah had one more question for Deke. "So what's with the hisses and grunts?"

"When Mrs. Cunningham was backing away from me, she got too close to the edge of the steps. I reached out to catch her before she fell off and broke something. The minute I touched her, she pepper-sprayed me. I've been hit with worse, but it stings pretty good."

Zachariah could imagine his practical, muscle-bound buddy being completely bamboozled by the woman's unpredictable behavior. He tried not to grin. "Was Mrs. Cunningham hurt?"

"I don't think so. After that, she ran to her car pretty fast. Locked herself inside. She's on the phone now. After what she accused me of, I don't think she's calling the cops."

Becky looked at her phone, looked straight across the restaurant at Zachariah, then turned away with a huff and answered the call. "No. She's not," Zachariah confirmed to Deke.

In one ear Zachariah listened to Becky explain who Deke was to Dimitra Cunningham, and that he was there to help gain evidence *against* Nick and to protect her and the house should Nick make a reappearance. "Go on back to school," Becky advised. "You and Nicky will be just fine."

In the other ear he heard Deke begging off his assignment. "You'd better get someone else to watch the lady, boss. There's no way she's going to trust me now."

"Dimitra," Becky was talking again. "You don't have to be alone in the house with Lieutenant Stahlnecker, but maybe you could bring him a damp cloth to wash his face. No, you don't have to stay. But I promise he's only there to protect you. No. He's not a friend of Nick's. All right. I'll meet you at the courthouse tomorrow."

Becky disconnected her phone and sent another pointed glare that spoke of just how much she thought Zachariah and his men were disrupting her work with all their precautions. He silently replied that he wasn't backing down one step, and neither were his men.

"She's getting out of her car," Deke whispered.

"I think you're stuck with the job," Zachariah advised. "Just keep your distance if she comes after you again."

"Very funny."

"Keep me posted if you see any sign of Cunningham on the premises."

"Will do. Stahlnecker out."

Armed with new information on Nick Cunningham and Roger Sligh that he could feed to Murphy once they got back to Becky's office, Zachariah clipped his phone back to his belt and asked the waitress for his bill. Though he wouldn't let down his guard until he got his hands around the throat of the bastard who wanted to hurt Becky, it made the mission a little less daunting to know they could narrow down the list of Joe Stalkers to only a handful of men Zachariah and his team needed to watch.

Speaking of…Zachariah watched as James Enderle

rose from his seat to kneel beside Becky's chair. *Sit your ass back down, pal. She can pick up her own napkin and put it back in her own lap. Get your damn hand off her thigh!*

Once Zachariah got Becky alone in a room where they didn't have to keep up this damn charade, they were going to have a little chat. Whether it was for her own safety or the salvation of their marriage, this game had a few rules she needed to follow.

She belonged to him. And though he wanted like crazy to shout that fact to the world, he respected her wishes to keep their marriage a secret. But their relationship was supposed to be progressing. They were supposed to be getting to know each other. Others should see them becoming a couple.

They weren't supposed to be having all these arguments and letting other men touch her and drift further and further apart from the magic that was them.

They were supposed to be falling in love.

Judging by the uncomfortable tightness squeezing his chest, Zachariah knew he was damn well following that last rule.

But was she?

"YOU'RE JEALOUS."

Becky climbed out of Zachariah's truck and headed down the sidewalk toward her office building. It didn't take a tall shadow falling over her shoulder and blocking the afternoon sun for her to know that Zachariah had fallen into step behind her. His tightly coiled energy alerted her long before his masculine scent teased her nose or his fingers brushed the small of her back.

"Yeah, well, if Mr. Grabby Hands understood the concept of a *business* meeting, I wouldn't have any reason to be, now would I?"

Becky grinned as she hastened her step to elude his touch in public where they might have an audience that could recognize them and mention something to her parents. "It's kind of cute that you're worried about James."

"I don't do *background* and I don't do *cute*. You have to respect that we made a commitment to each other. Even though I never got around to givin' you a ring, I haven't been with anybody else. I don't want to be with anybody else."

They paused for a crosswalk light and fell silent. As a group of pedestrians gathered to wait with them, she sensed that Zachariah took note of each and every person, quickly assessing whether or not someone stood too close to her or could pose any kind of threat. His attention lingered for a few seconds in one direction. His posture seemed to tighten, expand, but then forcibly relax as his searching gaze moved on. When the light changed, his fingers were on the strap of her bag, holding her back until the others had passed on by.

Was his almost obsessive need to see to her safety all about the guilt he'd mentioned yesterday in her office? A man he'd lost. *"…my fault. I tried to save him."* Or did he care about her so much that he couldn't stand to see her hurt? Was this bodyguard role about saving her or more about saving his own soul?

"I haven't been with anyone else, either," she whispered once they were walking again. "I do respect our vows. You didn't see *me* being Miss Grabby Hands, did you?" She glanced up to see herself reflected in the sunglasses he wore. "Did you?"

She couldn't read his eyes, but the corner of his mouth hitched, exposing a hint of a dimple along his jaw. "No."

"No, you didn't." *Good.* That was the closest thing she'd seen to a full-out smile since they'd made love at her apartment two nights ago. If Zachariah truly thought she'd been enjoying James's efforts to rekindle a romance that had never really gotten off the ground, then he was less observant than she'd been giving him credit for. "James has always been a touchy-feely kind of guy—shaking hands, kissing cheeks. It doesn't mean anything. And trust me, it has no effect on me." They reached the granite steps in front of her building and she darted up the first two ahead of him. As he came up behind her, she turned her cheek to his shoulder and whispered, "Not like when you touch me."

"You mean like this?"

Ooh. He ran a single finger up her spine, from waistband to nape, eliciting a shiver that radiated across her skin beneath her clothes.

"Zachariah!" She halted in her tracks, chiding him with a half-hearted reprimand. She hadn't seen this fun side to Captain Clark for a day and a half. She missed it. She missed him. She missed *them.* But throwing herself into his arms and encouraging him to finish what he started was out of the question. Not in broad daylight, not here in public. "Watch it," she mouthed.

"Oh, I'm watchin'," he answered.

When he gestured for her to proceed him up the steps, she had a feeling she knew exactly what he was watching.

"Back when James and I were dating, I kept waiting for the thrill to kick in, but it never did."

"Oh, that helps. You *dated* that clown?" He held open the front door for her and motioned her to one of the security checkpoints where she opened her attaché bag and he emptied his pockets and handed over the black steel pistol he wore at his back, along with his permit to carry it.

After being cleared by security, they gathered their things. "James Enderle's father has been friends with Dad since they went to college together. I think he always hoped that James and I would hit it off and become this unstoppable political couple. But I just couldn't stomach the thought of spending a lifetime with blond, bland and boring. So we decided to remain just friends." They headed to the bank of elevators. "You, big guy, are neither blond, bland nor boring."

"So there's hope for me yet, hmm?" He tucked his sunglasses inside his jacket, and Becky instinctively reached up to straighten his lapel. That slight smile reappeared, reaching his eyes now. He wagged a finger at her. "Uh-uh, Miss Owens. No touching. We're still getting to know each other, remember?"

She crossed her arms to keep her hands pinned beneath them and concentrated on the elevator's brass doors. "Well, if we're learning new things about each other, you should know that jealous, controlling men are a real turnoff for me. Now, a little minor possessiveness is sweet, but…" She tipped her chin so he could read the double meaning in her words. "Don't be jealous."

James Enderle means nothing to me.

Zachariah nodded—understanding, she hoped. Thankfully, he moved on to a new topic. "So, you like doing that kind of thing, Miss Owens? Planning parties? Raising money for candidates?"

"To paraphrase my father—what I like is helping my mother. Ralph Barclay is a big supporter of programs that fund breast cancer research and treatment. With my family history, I'm a supporter, too."

Elevator doors opened and a group of people filed out. As they stepped aside to let them pass, Zachariah slyly pointed to her breasts. "Is there any chance that you…?"

"There's been nothing to indicate that yet. I get regular exams and try to do the things that help prevent it. But it's caused by genetics as much as anything, so there's always a possibility." He followed her onto the elevator, looking a little concerned by that particular revelation. She reached in front of him to push the twelfth-floor button. "You said we had to get to know each other. The possibility of developing breast cancer is something I have to live with. You'd have to, as well. Could you handle being with a woman who has an above average chance of developing cancer at some time in her life?"

He waited long enough to answer that she looked up, and saw nothing but the outline of his jaw above her head. When he dipped his chin and met her gaze, she could see there was no teasing, no flirtation, no pretense in his answer. "Could you handle being with a man who disarms bombs, carries a gun and faces down the enemy for a living, and who, God forbid, would most likely have to go off to war again at some time in his life?"

Becky turned into his body and wrapped her arms around his waist. "We never talked like this before."

His deep breath matched her own and she snuggled closer to his hardness and warmth as his arms folded around her. "I want to do better by you next time we're apart. Keep in contact. I don't want to be…strangers every time I come home."

"Me, either." She drank in his warm masculine scent. His physical impression was already a vibrant memory. But there was still so much to learn about each other. "This is harder, isn't it? This is stuff, deeper inside, that we never got around to sharing. It's hard to talk about the parts of us that aren't so…strong."

She felt his lips at her temple. "Wanting you is easy. Needing you…"

Makes me vulnerable. "I know." For two wills as strong as theirs, accepting their own vulnerabilities— and allowing someone else to have access to that weakest part within them—might be the biggest hurdle of all. Becky turned her head, seeking his kiss. "I promise you, I take every precaution the doctor tells me to. But there are no guarantees."

His fingers were beneath her chin, angling her mouth toward his. "No guarantees here, either. But I'm incredibly well trained and I take every precaution I can, too."

Becky was vaguely aware of the number three lighting up in her peripheral vision. But every cell in her body was potently focused on Zachariah's hard mouth claiming hers.

By the time the four lit up, she'd pushed him against the back wall of the elevator and dropped her bag. Buttons were popping by five, and by six, she wasn't noticing the numbers anymore. "I need you."

Zachariah picked her up and stumbled across the elevator. "At your command."

He set her on the brass railing and pressed her back into the paneled wall. He speared his tongue into her mouth as he shoved her skirt up to her hips to slip his hand beneath her panties and squeeze a handful of her bottom. She tasted coffee and man and something sweet; but wanted more. Without loosening his tie, Becky plucked at the buttons of his shirt and found her way inside to sear her palms against hot skin and the supple muscles underneath. His abdomen spasmed beneath the sweep of her hands. She teased each male nipple into rock-hard nubs and he gasped her name.

He wedged his knee up between her thighs and Becky moaned as her weight concentrated pressure at the apex of her moist, sensitive opening. The almost painful pleasure pinpointed there made her fluid and heavy and primed for more. She braced one hand on his chest, the other on the bar beside her and rode his thigh, helplessly clasping her legs around him as he lifted her again and again.

"Zach…Zach…" She was floating, flying.

She nipped at his chin. He pushed his thumb

beneath the elastic of her panties and dragged it against her swollen folds. Her breath came in hard, quick gasps. He bounced her on his thigh one more time, then leaned in, pushing the hardness of his body into her aching center and driving her over the brink.

She was still feeling lightheaded with the speed and intensity of her climax when Zachariah lowered her to the floor. He planted one last quick kiss on her mouth before retreating to the far corner of the elevator where he began to button his shirt and tuck it back into his slacks. "I'll bet old *blond, bland and boring* never got your clock tickin' like that in just twelve floors."

"I guarantee you he didn't." Becky tugged her slip and skirt back into place. "I wish we had twelve more floors so I could return the favor."

"I can jam the buttons if you want."

The floating sensation had as much to do with the elevator slowing its ascent as it did the aftershocks still pulsing through her body. *Twelve more floors?* For the first time, she was thankful the building's elevators were on the slow side. "Oh, my God."

An old Zachariah grin split his face. "I enjoyed getting better acquainted with you, Miss Owens."

The number twelve lit up. She combed her fingers through her hair and pulled her jacket shut to mask what she hadn't had time to tuck in. "Maybe you should ask me out sometime, Mr. Clark. I'd say yes."

"I think you just did."

Becky laughed as the elevator car jerked to a stop. "Decorum, Mr. Clark. This is where I work. Put your ego back in your pants and pull yourself together or people will talk."

"Let them talk." There went the teasing banter. "This charade isn't working. Let's talk to your parents about us. Tell them about Cunningham. Let's quit hiding in elevators and hotel rooms and give ourselves a real chance."

"You know I can't…" The doors opened.

"Don't say it." Zachariah looped the bag she'd forgotten over her shoulder. The bodyguard was back. The husband in him was undoubtedly frustrated, most likely hurt. That made her hurt, too.

But he hid it all behind that tough-guy facade. Like she hid it behind her suit and icy exterior. One step closer to each other and two steps back.

"You're rumpled, Miss Owens."

She glanced behind her before blotting her smeared lipstick with her fingertips and stepping off the elevator. Mr. My-Way-or-the-Highway wasn't as pulled together as he seemed. "And you're unzipped, Mr. Clark."

IN HIS SIDE-VIEW MIRROR, he watched them both coming up the sidewalk across the street.

As soon as the Goliath looked away, he dropped his hand from the side of his face. He spared one longing glance at the mutilated photograph in his lap, then turned to look his fill of the real thing as the lights changed.

There she went, strutting her plump little ass over the crosswalk as though she owned the city. Tromping over men's egos probably gave her that inflated sense of importance that allowed her to hold her chin so high. Sure, she wore the right clothes that made her look conservative and professional. She said the right words that made her sound smart. But she was a spiteful bitch through and through. Undeserving of all she had—family, wealth, status.

Taking away what a man worked hard for—what a man deserved—gave her a taste of power she hadn't earned. She stuck her nose where it didn't belong, and made decisions that weren't hers to make. She made other women think they could stand up and screw over a man, too.

Well, Miss Becky Owens—he was going to put a stop to that.

He could tell he was getting to her. Oh, she tried to be all cool and prissy and act like he didn't. But he'd seen her at her client's house on Sunday, lured there as he'd planned by his violent catharsis from the night before.

When she'd run into the street to read his note, he could have taken her then. But he hated to stray from his well-constructed plan. He was controlling her life now—and he wasn't about to relinquish that control. Besides, watching her fear escalate had given him far too much pleasure. He'd sat back and watched her turning every which way and back, thinking she'd see him and confront him and put him in his place. Never again. She knew he had the upper hand now.

She knew it was *her* turn to pay.

His nostrils flared with a deep breath and he savored a rush of excitement in his loins. Hell, he had her so rattled that she'd hired a bodyguard for protection. Good.

He smiled, stroking his fingertip over his lips, thinking of all the deliciously wicked things he could do to her to destroy that ego, to rob her of that arrogance, to put her in her place for degrading him so. She thought she was in charge of her life, but he would be the one calling the shots in the end.

Hold on. "What's this?"

Becky and her bloodhound of a bodyguard had stopped on the steps leading up to the State Attorney's building. She was laughing. He was touching. Though she quickly pushed him away, Becky and her Goliath seemed to be a little friendlier with each other than an employer-employee relationship called for.

For a split second, he considered warning the man about all she would eventually take from him. But that would tip his hand. And Goliath didn't strike him as someone who would listen to reason, anyway.

No, the bodyguard was just another obstacle the bitch had thrown into his path. Perhaps having what she considered feelings for that man could work to his advantage. The bodyguard might be a challenge, but he could take him out, as well. *Before* he finished with Becky Owens. Let her feel the pain of loss the way he had. After she'd suffered, while she was down—*then* he'd finish his work.

He smiled. "Since you're upping the stakes in this game, so will I."

He turned and eyed the present on the seat beside him. He kissed his fingers, then touched them to the deadly gift.

So will I.

10

ZACHARIAH ROUSED HIMSELF the next morning and wondered if he was an idiot for getting so twisted up inside over a woman.

Now this mess with Becky was affecting his sleep.

He was tired and grouchy and hard as a rock for the woman sleeping in the room next to his. But hell, instead of a mere twenty feet, Becky might as well be miles away—with a wall, her parents, Joe Stalker and eighteen months' worth of secrets standing between them.

By the time he shipped out in a few weeks, he needed to have a better plan in place than an impulsive proposal and a "See you later." But his leave time was a ticking clock—he couldn't report back to the Corps until he knew his wife was safe. And until Becky and the rest of the world understood that she *was* his wife.

How the hell was he supposed to be a better husband the next time he was overseas when he couldn't even be a husband to her while they were sharing the same house?

Zachariah rolled over in bed and let his eyes adjust to the pearlescent light of dawn filtering through the sheer curtains at the window. This bedroom was bigger than his entire old base-quarters apartment had been. And hell, this was just the spare room. Well, one of them.

Like the rest of the sprawling Owens estate, this room had been decorated in what his mom would call "magazine style." Hardwood floors, lots of antique-lookin' furniture and knickknacks like Becky had at her place. Insulated glass, blinds and two types of curtains at the windows. He supposed if he cared about such things, it was a beautiful room. To look at— sure—he'd concede the class and comfort of the place.

But it was empty.

His bed was empty.

He was empty.

Carefully plucking the tangle of covers from between his legs, Zachariah sat up. "Ah, hell."

Maybe it was just as well that he suffer another morning of this soul-robbing emptiness alone. He sure as hell wasn't any kind of a catch when he felt like this. The nightmare must have hit him sometime in the night, judging by the wrinkled mess he'd made of the bed and the pillows he'd knocked to the floor.

But the burning vision of Darrell Watson's death had given way to an equally cruel kind of frustration. Memories and fantasies had blended together in his head to torment his slumber—images of Becky's bouncing breasts and clear blue eyes beckoning him. Her sweet lips on his cock. Her sassy commands in his ear. Her head thrown back in ecstasy as he watched her come with his hand or on his knee. Her lush, hot flesh welcoming him in a dozen different ways and places.

The soft press of her body as she wrapped his big frame up in a hug and gently touched his face with a promise of comfort he didn't deserve.

"Double hell."

He slid to the edge of the bed and slowly swung his legs over the side. The chaos of the fancy room and the tent at the front of his boxer shorts mocked his ability to cope with the tender feelings wreaking havoc inside him.

Zachariah raised his nicked-up, callused left hand and rubbed at the empty third finger with his thumb. He'd asked Becky to marry him in that D.C. hotel room for a reason—and not just because he wanted to claim her sexy self for him alone and keep the likes of James Enderle with those pretty-boy hands away from her. Six days wasn't a hell of a lot of time to know something for a fact, but he should have trusted his instincts with her the same way he used to trust his instincts on the battlefield.

He'd fallen in love with Becky Owens.

Now *that* was a hell of a thing to sneak inside a man's brain before he got his guard up in the morning.

He'd shown the Beckster how much he wanted her, but he'd done a lousy job of showing just how much he *needed* her. He hadn't let her into the dark places inside him. He hadn't let her see into his heart.

And now there was so much collateral damage between them that she might not even want to look. He might lose her. Not to Nick Cunningham or Roger Sligh or whoever Joe Stalker might be—he wouldn't allow that bastard anywhere near her.

He could lose her from his own inability to stand

up and tell her exactly what he felt. He was a man of action; he could make love to her those dozen different ways, he could put himself between her and a nutcase with a bomb. But he needed to step up and say the words. She needed to hear them. Believe them. Trust that she was more than an affair, more than a job, more than a salve for his battle-fatigued brain. He needed to put that ring on her finger to show her, himself, and anybody who'd listen, that he loved her.

Then pray to God he hadn't screwed things up so badly that she couldn't love him back.

He'd never have another peaceful night's sleep until he did.

Knowing what the problem was, however, wasn't the same as knowing what to do about it. Until he came up with a decent plan that wouldn't make things any worse, Zachariah intended to deal with the issues that he *could* handle. He could clean up the evidence of his nightmare, take a cold shower and get dressed so that he could get a jump-start on contacting Murphy and Deke to set up some extra security for Becky's appearance in court that morning. Today, she was representing Dimitra Cunningham in her final settlement and custody hearing. Zachariah wanted to finally get a good look at Nick Cunningham. He wanted to look deep into the bullying SOB's eyes to see if he could spot the enemy there.

With his jacket tossed over his shoulder and his tie loosely knotted around his neck, Zachariah stepped out into the hallway. He took the ten steps to Becky's room and stopped. He splayed his fingers at the center of the door and leaned in, listening for any sounds of waking—or wanting him.

The hour was early. The room was silent. The idea of stealing in and waking her with a kiss warmed his blood and sent it chugging through his veins.

But a more rational thought slammed the brakes on his libido and sent him on down the hall to the staircase. If he'd coached her right, independent Becky would wake with a scream at an unexpected man in her room, thus alarming her parents and triggering a whole slew of questions and accusations. He didn't want to get himself kicked out when she still needed a protector—he didn't trust that anyone else would be as committed to the job of keeping her safe as he was. Even if he managed to muffle her, preferably by covering her mouth with his own, there'd still be that awkward voice in his head, nagging the pleasure from the moment— *I want more than these clandestine rendezvous you're allowing me, Beckster. I need something more. Is there any chance you need more than that, too?*

If her answer was anything but a resounding yes, he'd be totally screwed. Zachariah Clark might be ready for battle, but he wasn't sure he'd ever be ready for another kind of heartbreak.

Zachariah circled the foot of the staircase and headed straight to the kitchen at the back of the house. Frederick, the butler dude who didn't say much but always seemed to know when someone needed something around there, had informed him that the cook, Delia, prepped a fresh pot of coffee for the staff each morning. As long as a good night's sleep continued to elude him, Zachariah would rely on the old Marine survival strategy of catnaps and caffeine to keep him alert when he was working near enemy lines.

He found the coffeemaker easily enough, and true to Frederick's word, the aroma of fresh-brewed beans gave his senses a jolt. But Zachariah never got around to filling his mug.

Before he reached the counter, he heard the chirping of birds echoing through the stillness of the empty kitchen and breakfast nook. The sound drew his gaze to the back exit. A slice of dappled sunlight poured through the crack where the curtained door stood slightly ajar. In a house where he was the only person making any noise that morning, his radar went on instant alert. Zachariah dropped his jacket over a stool and reached behind him to unholster his gun.

With Cunningham's police training, he'd know how to disable the estate's alarm system and get onto the property without passing through the front gate where Zachariah had left his name and picture so the guard could keep an eye out for him. If Nick Cunningham could trash his own former backyard to terrorize his ex-wife, he might be ballsy enough to try invading Becky's territory in an attempt to frighten and intimidate her. He might already be inside the house.

Only, a closer examination revealed no dewy tracks from the damp lawn on the linoleum. No sounds but the birds and the bubbling coffee. This wasn't a break-in. This was carelessness. With his initial alarm easing from red alert to mild caution, Zachariah lowered his .45 to his side and stepped out onto the patio to survey the garden, just in case his instincts were as off as they'd been the night of Corporal Watson's death.

He zeroed in on the woman at the glass-topped table, taking her breakfast beneath an arbor of grape vines. Sitting with her back to him, she hummed a tune along with the birds. Looked like someone who belonged here, not an intruder. Probably Frederick's Delia. Making a mental note to have a word with the staff about closing and locking doors, Zachariah turned to slip back into the house.

"Good morning, Mr. Clark." The woman called after him. "Is anything wrong?"

Zachariah turned to face her.

Ah, hell. *Way to go, Clarksie.* Even without an introduction, he could tell from the shape of that serene smile that this was Becky's mother. The invalid whose delicate health they were all lying to protect.

"Good morning, ma'am." Zachariah hid his gun behind his back and slipped it back into its holster as he approached her. "Uh, no, just a precaution." He'd better ask. "Are you alone out here?"

"I was." Her eyes drifted shut and she tipped her face to the gentle sunlight. "Just me and the music of the birds."

Great. Big man, big gun, creeping low and quick around the garden hedge. He was lucky he hadn't given the woman a heart attack.

"I saw the back door was open and thought I'd better check it out. Sorry to disturb you, ma'am." He retreated back toward the kitchen.

"Would you like to join me for a bite of breakfast

in the garden? It's lovely out here in the summer."
When he turned to make his excuses, her blue eyes
were open again and she held out her hand. "I'm Lily
Owens. We haven't had a chance to meet yet. I understand you're watching over my daughter."

"Zachariah Clark." He took the hand she offered,
cradling it lightly in his fingers, worried that its slender
boniness would snap in his grip. He could see why
Becky described her as fragile. She was pencil-slim
and small, swallowed up inside the sailing jacket she
wore. Her skin was as pale as Becky's, but there were
faint blue shadows under her eyes. Her hair was only
about a quarter inch longer than his own, but it was as
white as the snowy flowers blooming in the hedge.

Despite the older woman's frailties, though, he recognized a brain as sharp as Becky's. Mama wasn't supposed
to know about any crank calls or hiring a bodyguard. As
far as Bertram and Becky had told her, he was here to
oversee security for Senator Barclay's reception.

"No thanks, ma'am. I was just lookin' for coffee."

"Delia has a fresh pot right here." She picked up a
mug from the breakfast tray at the center of the table
and poured a cup. She set it in front of the chair beside
her. "I'd appreciate the company, unless you have to
run off with my daughter."

Yeah, um, that was an awkward choice of words.

"Miss Owens isn't going to the office today. She has
court later this morning." He thumbed over his
shoulder. "There's coffee in the kitchen. I can entertain myself while I'm waitin' for her."

Lily waved aside the idea. "You'll be entertaining

yourself for an hour or more, then. She's just like her father. Neither one of them is a morning person by nature. Probably because they try to get too much done during the day. Night owls, both of them. I can't tell you how many mornings I've had breakfast by myself over the years. Normally, I appreciate the peace and quiet. But I've had far too much of that lately." She pointed to the chair beside her. "Sit. You're giving me a crick in my neck."

"Sorry, ma'am." Zachariah pulled back the wrought-iron seat and sank onto the dark green cushion. "Maybe I could stay for just one cup."

Zachariah was beginning to think he was dealing with a ringer here. Deceptively fragile on the outside, but strong of spirit. Lily Owens was a closet tough chick. Dainty and petite, sure, he could tell she'd been struggling with her illness.

But no sooner had he picked up his drink than she pushed a plate of food in front of him—eggs, cinnamon rolls, slices of ham, fresh fruit. "Eat. I know the kind of snacks Delia puts out in the morning for the staff. They won't fill up a strong young man like you. And she always serves me far too much. I think she gives me a little of everything to make sure there'll be something on the plate that will whet my appetite."

He found the corner of his mouth curving into a smile. *Sit. Eat.* The commands she gave sounded pleasantly familiar—friendly suggestions that gave him permission to do what he really wanted to. "Much obliged, ma'am. I went straight from mess hall meals and MREs to restaurants and room service. It's nice to get a taste of home-cooked food."

The smile that lit her face reminded him of Becky during those first six days together. Before the war. Before the threats. Before this damn charade.

"The thanks go to Delia. But I'm glad to see the food isn't going to waste this morning." She sat and watched him eat several bites before she asked, "Do you dance, Mr. Clark?"

"I'm passable. My mother made my brother and sisters and me all learn how. Nothing fancy, though."

"What kind of music do you like?"

"If you're askin' whether or not I'll be waltzing at the reception on Saturday—I can't. I'll be workin'." But that wasn't what she'd asked, and her annoyed expression told him so. The woman wasn't projecting into the future or worrying about the past. She wanted to be in the moment. She just wanted to talk. "Country, ma'am."

"I always wanted to sing like Patsy Cline myself, but I quickly learned that my talents lay more in the instrumental area."

"Yeah? What instrument do you play?"

He polished off the eggs and she pushed a cup of yogurt and some granola his way. "Several. Piano. Flute. Banjo…"

Zachariah was stuffed to the gunwales and laughing along with Lily when the patio door opened. He didn't have to turn to know who was behind him. He recognized Becky's exotic perfume and his pulse instantly quickened. "Good morning, Mom."

"Good morning, dear."

"How did you sleep? Are you warm enough?" As mother and daughter exchanged a morning hug and health report, Zachariah returned his plate and utensils to the serving tray and stood. Time to resume the charade. When Becky tipped her chin toward him, her polite smile was as brittle and forced as Lily's had been warm and inviting. "Zachariah. Could I see you inside for a minute?"

He nodded dutifully. He knew what was comin', and he didn't care one damn bit. He may have resisted sitting down in the first place, but he'd enjoyed his breakfast and his company, and he wasn't going to apologize for it. With a nod to Lily, he excused himself. "Thanks for breakfast, ma'am."

"I'm up early every day, Mr. Clark. You're welcome to join me as long as you're here."

He grinned. "See you in the mornin'."

Becky clutched his arm as soon as the door closed behind him and tugged him into the kitchen. The false smile had vanished. "What were you doing out there?"

"Making nice with the mother-in-law." Zachariah easily twisted his arm from her grasp and went back to retrieve his suit coat and pull it on. "You never know when you're going to need brownie points with her."

"Not when she doesn't *know* she's your mother-in-law."

"Fine. I had breakfast with my boss's mother. She knows I've got a thing for Martina McBride and that I prefer my eggs over easy. Did you know either of those things about me?"

Now that he had his sleeves and collar adjusted

comfortably, he slowly followed her urgent retreat into the front entryway.

"This isn't about us, it's about protecting her. We're easing her into the you and me possibility. As far as she knows, we've just met. Remember?"

Ouch. He stopped. "We're just a *possibility* now?"

"Don't put words in my mouth." She snatched up her bag from the front table.

"Then say what you mean."

"Fine." Becky whirled around. She marched right up to him and poked a finger at the center of his chest. "Stay away from my mother. Number one, she's supposed to be resting this week, not serving you breakfast and entertaining the troops. And two, you don't know the intuition that woman possesses. If you give her too much opportunity to observe and analyze us, she'll know that we're hiding something from her."

"I think you're sellin' her short, darlin'. Her body may be weak, but there's not a thing wrong with that brain of hers. I didn't say a word and she knew that I'm here specifically to protect you, not work the party. Did you or your dad say anything?"

"I didn't. And I'm sure Dad wouldn't." His defensive anger eased as she twisted her fingers into his lapel. "I don't want you taking a risk like that. I'm not ready for her to find out about us. I want it to be a good surprise, not something she feels regret over or worries about."

He wanted to pull Becky into his arms and hold her until that fearful anxiety left her eyes. But she didn't want to be held. Not here. Not by him. So he gently pulled her hand from his chest and moved around her to open the door.

"You're not ready for anyone to find out—"

"Could we not start that again this morning?" She dashed past him and hurried down the front steps. "I have to be in court in an hour. I can't mess this up today. Dimitra's counting on me."

Zachariah pulled the door shut and followed her down to her car. "Fine. I'll shut up. But I'm meeting Lily for breakfast again tomorrow. She's awake when I am. She's pleasant company. She has coffee. And she's the one person in this house who isn't living a lie."

WITH AN ENTOURAGE OF THREE Marines either leading the way or following behind her and her client, Becky pushed open the doors of the courtroom and stepped into the marbled hallway.

"Congratulations, Dimitra. You won." She hugged the slender woman, then pulled back to see the first hint of a hopeful smile softening her face.

"So he cannot take the house or Nicky away from me?"

Becky shook her head. "And if he falls behind in his alimony or child support again, the State will automatically garnish his wages. Failure to comply with the court order could affect even his supervised visitations with Nicky."

Taking note of the people moving up and down the hall, Thomas Murphy chimed in. "In other words, Mr. Nick better mind his manners or there'll be hell to pay."

"Murphy." Deke's gruff voice reprimanded his friend.

Murphy winked at Dimitra. "I didn't mean anything by that, ma'am. Congratulations. I hope everything works out for you and the kid."

"Thank you." Though a little bamboozled by Murphy's charm, and more than a bit shy around the bulk of Zachariah and Deke, Dimitra nonetheless turned to each man, looking them straight in the chin. "Thank you all for helping me."

Rather than trading thanks, Zachariah was more interested in the muffled voices they could hear through the thick wooden door behind them. Nick Cunningham wasn't the only Richmond police officer who'd shown up for the hearing. George Wesley and a pair of internal-investigation officers had been on hand to observe the case. Without sufficient evidence to prove he was behind the threats to herself and Dimitra, Becky didn't know if there would be any criminal charges filed against him. But a stern talking-to from the big boss couldn't hurt.

Squat, boxer-built Deke, however, had plenty of attention to spare for Becky's pretty, dark-haired client. He still sported a red rash around his nose, cheeks and left eye from the burn of Monday's pepper spray. His straight mouth worked around a smile almost as awkward as Dimitra's. "It was nothin', ma'am. We were glad to help."

Dimitra's gaze stayed firmly fixed on Deke's square chin. "Thank you, too, for cleaning my yard, Mr. Stahlnecker."

Becky hid a smile as even more pink surfaced beneath Deke's rash. "Yeah, well, it needed to be done."

It would be a long time before Dimitra Cunningham would be ready to risk another relationship with a man. But from the look of things, it might take Deke about that long to work up the nerve to ask her out.

"May I walk you to your car, ma'am?" Deke asked.

"I—" Dimitra turned her startled look to Becky. "I rode with Miss Owens."

A *long* time before Dimitra would be ready for a relationship. Becky draped her arm around the other woman's shoulder and rescued her. "Why don't we all walk out to the parking lot together?"

Becky had barely taken a step when the courtroom door burst open and Nick Cunningham stormed out. A handsome, trim man of six feet, he wore his departmental uniform and a murderous scowl that flushed his face with anger. "You sneaky little foreign bitch."

"Mr. Cunningham," Becky snapped. "I'll ask you not to address my client."

Even as Becky turned away with Dimitra, Zachariah angled himself in front of Nick. "Back off, Cunningham."

"You think you've hit the gravy train, don't you, D?" Nick twisted around Zachariah's warning hand and charged straight at his ex. "You've got my house, my money, my son—"

The blinding efficiency of a trained Marine taking down a man while two others moved innocent civilians out of harm's way was a thing to behold.

In mere seconds Becky was clutching at the band of Murphy's arm across her stomach, catching her breath.

Dimitra, even though she'd yelped at the unexpected contact, was out of sight behind the wall of Deke Stahlnecker's chest.

Nick Cunningham was flat on his face, cursing into the marble floor, his arms twisted behind him with Zachariah's knee pinning him at the small of his back.

"So much for anger management class," Murphy quipped.

No one laughed. But it eased the tension of the moment enough to make Becky aware of the audience standing in the courtroom's open doorway.

Police Chief George Wesley flashed his badge and waved off the building guards who were running up to take control the situation. He was flanked on either side by the Internal Affairs officers George had introduced her to earlier, before the hearing.

Cunningham's lawyer, a competent-enough attorney, was left with the unenviable task of hurrying forward to protect his client. "I demand you release Mr. Cunningham at once, sir. Before I file assault charges against you."

In one fluid motion, Zachariah rolled to his feet, pulling Nick up with him. He shoved the outmaneuvered cop into his attorney. "Not unless I press charges first." He nodded at the lawyer. "You keep him away from these women." He turned that same narrow-eyed warning on Cunningham. "Stay away."

"Bring it on, big man." Nick bumped his chest against his attorney's back, knocking the older man forward.

Zachariah didn't budge an inch. "Do you really want to take a swing at me?"

Using his lawyer's urging as a handy excuse, Nick wisely retreated. Instead of taking on Zachariah, he pointed an accusing finger at Becky. "This is your fault. Dimitra knew her place. She understood the order of things before you came along."

With one step, Zachariah blocked her view of Nick. "Point your finger at her again and I'll break it."

There was a beat of silence before a breathy huff of air told her Cunningham had relented.

Becky pushed aside Murphy's arm and moved up beside Zachariah. Not as close as she would have liked, though. Whatever dangerous energy had forced Nick Cunningham back still lingered in the air around him. "Are you all right?" she asked, not really expecting an answer.

None came. Zachariah the bodyguard was too intent, too focused to deal with any concern for himself.

"I believe this has turned into a police matter, gentlemen." George Wesley stepped forward, the calm authority of his presence getting through to Zachariah where she could not. She finally saw her husband breathe. His shoulders expanded and then relaxed.

Sort of. At least he finally turned his focus away from Nick. "Yes, sir."

"Officer Cunningham, I believe I'll have you come with me." George nodded to the two I.A. investigators.

"This ain't right. You can't bring my boss down on me."

"But I can," George answered. "Richmond PD is one of the most respected police forces in the country. I won't have one bad apple spoil our reputation for all of us. I'd like you to come downtown with us and answer a few questions."

"Should I bring my lawyer with me?"

George looked to the lawyer, then to Becky before addressing Cunningham again. "That's probably a good idea."

While the two I.A. men escorted Nick Cunningham toward the back door and parking lot adjacent to the building, Chief Wesley spared a glance at Zachariah and his compatriots. "I'm a former Navy officer myself. I appreciate you stepping in as concerned citizens for Miss Owens and Mrs. Cunningham's welfare. But I trust I won't see that sort of violence from any of you again in my city?"

"No, sir," Deke and Murphy answered together.

Chief Wesley raised his dark eyes to Zachariah, waiting for a response.

Finally, it came. "No, sir. Unless extreme circumstances call for it."

"Of course. Nicely done, gentlemen." He shook each man's hand, nodded to Dimitra and kissed Becky's cheek. "I'll leave you in good hands, then."

"Thank you." She gratefully returned the kiss. "Keep me posted on Nick Cunningham."

"Will do. I'll see you the night after tomorrow."

Once Chief Wesley and the other officers were on their way out the door, Zachariah nodded over the top of Becky's head to Murphy. "Head on back to Becky's office. I still want a twenty-four-hour monitor on the line there and on her home phone in case any more calls come in."

"Yes, sir." Murphy jogged on ahead of them.

Becky fell into step beside Zachariah, with Dimitra following close at her elbow. Deke brought up the rear.

"Won't the calls stop now that they've taken Nick away?"

"I don't know, darlin'." He twisted his head back and forth as if he was loosening a stiff neck. But his tension was mental, not physical. "Sorry. I mean, Miss Owens."

He walked right beside her, but the distance between where they'd started back in D.C. and where they were now felt like an insurmountable gulf. "Things will get better now," she promised. "I'll be able to concentrate on us. We can sit down and talk, and come up with a better plan. With a timetable so you'll know how seriously I want to make us…" She spared a glance at Dimitra who fell back a step to avoid eavesdropping. Becky tilted her chin up to the stern man beside her. "I want us to work. I want to tell people about us."

When the time is right.

She didn't have to say the words. Zachariah already knew them by heart.

He held open the door for her. "Let's just get home."

Becky pulled out her ring of keys and donned her sunglasses as they descended the back steps and crossed the street to the parking lot. Murphy honked his horn and waved as he drove away, and in the first row of reserved parking, she saw George Wesley and the I.A. detectives handcuff Nick Cunningham beside their unmarked police car.

Zachariah saw everything, too. But while Becky's

spirits seemed to lighten with a renewed hope in the early afternoon sunshine, Zachariah's wary mood seemed to grow darker and more introspective.

What had happened to the fun-loving Marine who looked at her with such desire? Who made her laugh? Made her forget every rule of common sense and decorum in her lonely, by-the-book life, and fall scarily, passionately in love with him?

Becky stumbled as the last revelation fell into place inside her head. She felt Zachariah's hand at her elbow, instantly steadying her. Steadying her, protecting her…loving her. Zachariah had given her everything—his body, his wit. He'd put his life on the line, and maybe he'd even put his heart out there for her, too.

During those six days in D.C., there hadn't been time to learn the extent of Zachariah's sense of honor. She hadn't completely understood that he would risk his life for a cause, for his country, for someone he believed in. She hadn't realized how deeply this big man's equally big heart could feel.

But she'd sensed it.

She'd married him because she'd sensed that he was more than a bed partner. He was everything she wanted.

But after the secrets and lies, the threats and danger, the mistakes and hurtful words between them, how could she make him believe that she loved him? After all those months apart it had been too easy to build walls, to place blame, to make excuses. As strong and independent as she appeared—as circumstances had forced her to be—how did she convince him that she needed him? That he made her vulnerable in a way Nick Cunningham's sick threats never could?

What if she *couldn't* convince him that it was need, not just want, that she felt for him?

Becky's mood crashed and burned. She couldn't solve anything here. She needed to go home. She needed some time alone. She needed to think.

Tugging her elbow from his grasp drew Zachariah's attention away from Nick Cunningham and the police. "C'mon. My sardine can is just a couple of rows over. You can lock me in, and then I'll wait for you to pull up in your truck so you can follow me home."

"You should have let me drive you."

"Face it, Zachariah, even though she knows you're one of the good guys, Dimitra is terrified of you. Can you imagine the three of us squished together in the cab of your pickup? She'd have been a nervous wreck by the time we got to court. I had to drive her separately."

With the tension between us, I needed some distance from you, too.

"I'm not a complete bastard. I'm glad you won the case for her. But I'd like to get you home, where I have a better chance of guaranteeing your safety."

"Internal Affairs is taking Nick Cunningham away. You heard the threats he made. He has to be Joe Stalker. Give yourself a break." She pointed her keyless remote at her Nissan. "I think you can ease up on the worry."

Chirp-chirp.

Becky's eyes widened at the ball of bright light that bloomed beneath the hood of her car.

"Shit." Zachariah reacted a split-second sooner. He slammed his arms around her and spun as a roar of superheated air threw them to the ground.

The impact as she hit the ground, sandwiched as she was between man and concrete, bruised her lungs and robbed her of breath. Her right leg burned from knee to ankle, and her palms stung. Zachariah shielded her with his body as chunks of glass and metal and fire rained down.

An eternity passed in seconds before Zachariah eased himself off her back and rolled over beside her. Becky sucked in her first painful gasp of air. She pushed herself up onto her hands and knees, her brain processing all that was happening around her in disjointed bits and pieces.

People were screaming, running, pointing.

Her right leg was bleeding. She was missing a shoe.

Deke and Dimitra were huddled behind a car. He was helping her to her feet.

A shred of burning car part smacked the concrete beside her, and she jerked.

Zachariah's hands roamed over her in a hard, quick exploration. She could see his lips moving, *"Are you all right? Are you hurt?"*

Then she was sitting on her bottom and his raw knuckles moved along her injured leg as he plucked her torn stocking from the scraped-up skin.

It was maybe a minute before her brain kicked in and her ears unplugged to the sound of laughter. Cold, heartless, wicked laughter.

"Payback's a bitch, ain't it, lady?"

Nick Cunningham swallowed his laugh the instant Zachariah rose to his feet. He backed into the fender of the investigators' car, desperately searching for a hiding place as Zachariah's long legs ate up the distance between Becky and the reckless cop.

"Zachariah!" she shouted, ignoring the stiff ache of her body as she climbed to her feet to try to stop the looming disaster. "I'm all right! Zachariah—stop!"

Deke moved faster than Becky, reaching his buddy before he could get his hands on Nick. There was a brief struggle. "Captain! It's Deke. You gotta stop."

Zachariah shook off Deke's muscled grip and stumbled a few steps away.

As Becky limped up to him, she heard George Wesley on the phone, calling in the explosion. "...need a bus, a TAC unit and some crowd control behind the courthouse on 7th." He shifted his attention to Zachariah. "Son? You all right? Mr. Clark?"

But Becky could see Zachariah wasn't hearing the police chief at all. His blank eyes and harsh expression told her he was thousands of miles away, in a war zone where one of his men had died. Along with his ability to forgive himself....

11

THE NIGHTMARE PLAYED IN HIS mind and showed Zachariah a whole new glimpse of hell.

"Where the hell...? Watson! Fall back! Fall back!"

"I can reach it, sir!"

"Negative! We regroup now!"

"Just one more second."

"Get your ass out of there, Marine! It's gonna blow!"

"I almost—"

"Becky!"

Zachariah was gritty and greasy, slick with sweat. His nostrils burned from the fiery heat raining down around him.

But night had turned to day.

Desert fatigues had become a suit and tie.

Where was the clay hut with the battered car?

Where were his men?

Where the hell was Watson?

Zachariah groaned in his sleep, thrashing from side to side, willing himself to wake up.

But he was in too deep. The punishment for failure was never waking up. He wrestled with the demons who laughed at his pain.

"Payback's a bitch, ain't it, lady?"

No. Please. Stop.

But the demons weren't listening.

Doctors could patch up his shrapnel wounds. Paramedics could treat his cuts and scrapes.

But there wasn't medicine enough in the world to change the images in his head.

It wasn't Darrell Watson's slack body he carried in his arms this time.

It was Becky's.

Her clothes torn, her leg bloodied. A swath of black grease in her golden hair, her blue eyes unseeing.

The bastard had hurt her. He'd made good on his word. And like that fiery night in Al-Bazan, he'd been too late to save her.

Help me. Hell, no. He didn't want to see this.

"Becky!" He roared in his sleep, desperate to escape the cruel transfiguration of his memories.

Zachariah stood guard over a casket and watched Becky's mother cry.

The casket was open. Becky lay inside, pale and still. He'd lost her. He'd lost her.

Don't go. Don't leave me. I need you.

I need you.

I need.

"Zachariah." An angel's voice.

"Don't take her." The demons were coming to steal her from him. "Damn it, don't take her!"

"Zachariah!" An angel who couldn't stay with him.

He reached for his wife, the woman he loved. "Darlin'."

They wrestled with him, they tried to pin him down. He had to save her. He had to save Becky.

They pushed. He pushed back harder.

"You can't have her. She's mine!"

"SHE'S MINE!"

Becky froze beneath Zachariah's weight pressing her down into the bed.

She tried to call out his name a third time, but his forearm was wedged against her throat. She'd snuck into his room when she'd heard him crying out in wordless agony in his sleep. She'd tried to wake him, tried to free him from the awful trap of his nightmare.

When words hadn't worked she touched his shoulder and shook him. With little difference from the way he'd taken Nick Cunningham down at the court-house, Zachariah had picked her up and flipped her onto the bed. Trapped, as though she were the enemy inside his head.

In the hazy light from the moon outside, his eyes above her opened, red-rimmed and wild.

And she couldn't draw in a breath. *"Zachariah."*

He blinked a half-dozen times, quickly scanned the room, then looked down at her.

"Can't breathe."

His eyes narrowed, assessing her face. Identifying her?

Slowly he pulled back his forearm and Becky sucked in a blessed lungful of air. She inhaled and exhaled two more times, because there was little else she could do in this vulnerable position.

Even clad in nothing more than a pair of boxer shorts, he was a frightening, fierce warrior. But she also knew him to be a generous, tender lover.

She had to reach him. She needed to get through to the good, gentle man locked up inside.

"Are you awake?" she whispered, praying she'd see the light of conscious recognition spark in his eyes. "You were having the nightmare again. Do you know me?"

"Becky?" His racing heart pounded against her chest. His deep, ragged breaths pushed her deeper into the bed.

She nodded.

"You're alive?"

"Yes. I'm right here. I'm fi—"

Zachariah blotted out her answer with a grinding kiss. His midnight growth of beard rasped against her chin. His tongue snaked into her mouth.

When she tried to kiss him back, he went still.

"Oh, shit. And I've got you like this?"

She became aware again of his hands bearing down on her shoulders, her legs spread and pinned beneath his thighs—her body trembling and open and helpless beneath the heavy weight of him crushing her from breast to toe.

He scrambled off her almost as quickly as he had pinned her down. He slid all the way to the far side of the bed, planting his feet on the floor, bracing his elbows on his knees and dropping his face into the cradle of his hands.

"Oh, God, darlin', I'm sorry. We're in Virginia, right? At your parents' house?"

"Yes." Becky crawled over beside him, curling her

legs beneath her and adjusting her white gown over her lap. "It's not quite one in the morning."

He raked his fingers back across his scalp and rubbed his cheeks, roughly dispelling the last of his terrors. "And you're in my room? I thought you wanted us to have separate quarters."

Becky debated whether to move closer to comfort him, or move farther away for her own safety. He was raw and edgy and dangerous to touch. But in the end, she rallied her courage and listened to her heart. She inched closer and lay her hand against his bare shoulder, carefully avoiding the scattershot of tiny cuts that dotted his upper back after this afternoon's explosion.

He flinched beneath her touch. But after a moment, when he didn't pull away, she gently stroked her fingertips across his shoulder, almost petting him. She wanted him to know he was safe. He was cared for. "You cried out in your sleep. Like before."

She wanted him to know *she* was safe and that he could turn off his obsessive need to protect—to make things right for the young life he felt he hadn't protected well enough. Nick Cunningham was in police custody for making threats, even though he'd insisted he hadn't carried out any of them. Hell, he could have been killed by that car bomb, too, he'd argued.

No one had been seriously injured, thank God, but her car had been destroyed.

Her confidence had been shaken to the bone.

And Zachariah's troubled conscience had taken a direct hit.

Becky climbed up onto her knees, balancing her

weight to take the pressure off the abraded and bandaged skin along her right knee, calf and ankle. Keeping her touch as gentle as she could make it, she cupped the back of his head and slowly stroked his short, crisp hair. "I heard you even through the wall in my room. I couldn't stand to let you suffer."

"I'm all right now. You can go back."

He swallowed hard and she watched the play of muscle and sinew at the sides of his neck. Becky moved her gentle massage farther down, using both hands now to rub the knots of stress in the juncture where his neck angled out to his shoulders. Her voice was as quiet as the hushed night outside the room. "I'm not leaving you."

For several minutes she worked the kinks from his muscles, which were as stiff and sore from the turmoil inside him as much as from their flying dive to the pavement this afternoon. Just as her own fingers began to tighten, the balls of tension unknit themselves and his shoulders lifted in a heavy sigh—like a big jungle cat stretching as it awoke.

But just as quickly, he shrugged off her touch and scooted to the end of the bed, damning himself with every word. "I had you spread-eagled on the bed and completely at my mercy. I could have choked the life out of you. I'm no better than Cunningham."

"No." Becky crawled after him. She matched his position, sitting up and dangling her legs over the side, though her feet didn't touch the floor. "The Zachariah Clark I know would never hurt me. You're not well. You weren't yourself."

"That's a lousy excuse. I thought you were the enemy. I treated you like—"

"You didn't hurt me."

"Liar."

"You startled me, yes. But you didn't hurt me."

He turned his head, then reached out to brush aside a tendril of hair from her cheek. "You're sure?"

She nodded, leaning into his touch until he pulled away. No. He couldn't really believe he'd abused her, could he?

Becky scooted off the bed and came to stand between his knees. She caught his scruffed chin in her hand and tilted his face to look deep into the sad guilt haunting his eyes. "I am not a victim. Never have been. Never will be. I'm too mule-headed to ever stand for that kind of thing in my life. Or haven't you learned that about me yet?"

It wasn't yet a smile, but the deep grooves bracketing his mouth softened. "You'd come after me with a baseball bat if I tried to hurt you, wouldn't you?"

She did smile. "I'd at least come after you with a court order."

Zachariah moved his hands to her waist, resting them at the curve of her hips but not truly holding on to her. "I'm a big SOB, darlin'. I could do some damage even if I didn't mean to. I couldn't forgive myself if I ever hurt you or frightened you the way I saw Dimitra lookin' at Cunningham this mornin'."

Becky's grip on his jaw tightened. Her tone grew stern. "Don't ever compare yourself to Nick Cunningham again. He's a coward. People have choices. He chose to abuse his wife because it made him feel like he was stronger than somebody, like he was a man for having that kind of power. Instead of fixing what was wrong in his life, he took it out on her." She gentled her touch, traced the line of his buzz-cut hair around his face and pressed her thumb against his bottom lip. "You are no coward. I think it must take a very brave man to carry the memories of all you've been through and shoulder the responsibility for the men and women in your command—and still laugh and charm and make sweet, wonderful love to me."

His fingers tightened at her hips. He was holding her now. "Do you think I woke your parents?"

She stroked her thumb across his lips, coaxing the beginnings of a smile. "They'd be here by now if you had. They're at the far end of the hall on the opposite side of the landing."

"So you snuck into my room under your parents' noses. That's kind of teenagery of you." His mouth widened with a full-fledged grin. "That's kind of hot. Maybe you'd better go back to your room before I get you in trouble."

She appreciated his effort to make her smile. But she wouldn't let him push her away and pretend the nightmare had never happened. Not this time.

"Do you want me to go?"

The grin faded, and Zachariah couldn't seem to speak. Then he shook his head no, wrapped his arms behind her waist and pulled her in to bury his face between her breasts. He hugged her hard, inhaling the scent at her cleavage, nestling his grizzled cheek against the soft swells. He shook his head again.

Becky slid her hands behind his neck and held him close to her heart. "Then I'm here. I'm yours. Any way you want me."

"You'll stay?" he whispered, kissing her breast as he spoke.

"If you want me to."

"No. I *need* you to." He reached for the hem of her nightgown and leaned back enough to pull it off over her head. Then he fell back against the covers, pulling her on top of him, holding her tight, one hand on her butt, the other in her hair. "I need you to stay with me."

He simply held her like that for several minutes and Becky felt the gentle rise and fall of his chest. The air conditioning was cool at her back, but her temperature was rising degree by degree from this simple skin-to-skin contact with Zachariah.

Once he was assured that she wasn't going to leave him tonight, the tension in his body eased and the atmosphere in the room began to change. It grew sultry and close. The outside world faded away, leaving Becky and Zachariah cocooned in a bubble of need and desire. He framed her face, kissing her once, twice. Denying her a third kiss to speak. "I need you to have your way with me. Whatever you want to do to me. It's only fair to give you the advantage after scaring the crap out of you."

"You don't owe me anything."

"I need to let you do this. I need to…surrender control."

"You want me to seduce you?"

"It doesn't have to lead to that."

But they both knew it would.

Ignoring the sting in her leg as she shifted her weight, Becky knelt on the bed beside him. She felt a little shiver of anticipation, a little jolt of humility at the power he was handing over to her. "Anything?"

He squeezed her hand before spread-eagling himself on the center of the bed. "I'm at your command."

Thank God for the moon and security lights outside the window. For a few moments, all she could do was sit there and study him. Zachariah's eyes watched her intently, but he held himself still beneath her scrutiny, except for the deep, long breaths that lifted his chest.

He lay there, a big, primal male specimen—rangy, muscular, tanned all the way down to the waistband of his boxers, and again from the hem down to his toes. Every inch, every muscle, was completely at her mercy.

That gift—that trust alone—was enough to make her squeeze her thighs together against the ribbon of warmth that spiraled deep inside her.

After looking her fill, Becky began to touch. Just a curious inspection of the things that made him uniquely a man, uniquely Zachariah. She drew her fingertips along the thick, corded sinews of his thighs. She examined the dimple beside each knee, teased her palms over the crisp, curling, fawn-colored hair on his legs. She discovered he was ticklish beneath the curve of his toes, and although he clenched them at the overly sensitive touch and possibly wanted to play the same game with her, one look from Becky and he dutifully stilled.

His breathing quickened ever so slightly and his nostrils flared as she shifted positions and turned her exploration to other parts of his body. She took note of the bulge swelling at the front of his shorts, but chose to ignore that temptation for now. Instead, she traced the flat of his stomach along the elastic waist of his boxers, smiling when she brushed another sensitive spot and he sucked in his gut.

But he couldn't get away from her touch that easily.

With a throaty laugh, she dipped her finger into his bellybutton and swished it around one, two, three times. When he wanted to laugh, she shushed him, and when he limited himself to a smile, she rewarded him with a kiss at that ticklish spot. Then Becky moved higher, over the muscled swell of each finely honed muscle that covered his ribs until she cupped the firm rise of each pectoral with the heel of her palms.

He was so well-built, so big, so fine. Every cell she touched heated beneath her hands. She looked up to find his deep, verdant gaze locked on her face, studying every reaction she had. She almost made him close his eyes so that he could respond to her through touch alone. But she couldn't deny herself the pleasure of their beautiful color or the myriad sensations reflected there.

She watched his eyes darken as she swirled her fingertips around his flat, bronze nipples. She watched his nose crinkle when she gently pinched the turgid little buttons between her thumb and forefinger.

A groan vibrated beneath her fingers as she splayed her hands flat, marveling at the distinct contrast of her fair skin against his darker, golden tone. Becky's own breath caught and she wriggled her shoulders into a new position to ease the ache that was pooling in the tips of her breasts. Zachariah's gaze darted to her breasts as she stretched, and she held them up proudly as he watched the aureoles swell and nipples pearl into aroused nubs.

His quick, deep breath drew her attention back to his body. Back to the four-inch pucker of scar tissue on his left flank. Knowing he'd been hurt, maybe in the same explosion that had killed the young corporal whose death haunted his dreams, triggered an ache inside Becky that was different from the pleasure unfurling inside her.

She touched the scar and he flinched.

"Don't." His voice was a croaking whisper.

Becky moved the finger to his lips. "Shh. You said anything."

Closing his eyes, he turned his head away as she touched the healed wound again. Then she shifted back on her knees, bent forward and kissed the mark.

"Ah." His whole body constricted.

She kissed it again, running her tongue against his skin. He twisted on the bed, but didn't move away or try to stop her. "What happened here?" she asked.

"Car bomb." Talking seemed to be difficult for him. She kissed it again. "Shrapnel wound."

"And here?" She moved to the tattoo on his bicep— the Marine Corps symbol, where another scar gave his proud eagle a wounded wing.

"Same explosion. Late at night. We tried to defuse it. It was too late."

Becky kissed the scar. He was harder here, against

the bulge of muscle. Becky massaged the arm, but he was tight. And getting tighter. "Relax."

But it was a command he couldn't obey.

Her heart warmed at his intense will. He'd promised to let her have her way with him. And no matter what it cost him—whether it was denying himself the expression of a physical need, or corralling the demons inside him so that she'd understand he'd never hurt her—he was going to let her be the one in ultimate control this night.

She had no intention of getting out a whip or chaining him up. But there were other ways she could have the stronger hand. Other ways her strength could take over his and grant him the reprieve he needed.

With a bold new confidence and a plan that made her own pulse jump in anticipation, she issued an order. "Roll over."

She accepted the trust he warily surrendered and vowed to make this as good for him as she intended it to be for her.

Quickly pulling his shorts off him and tossing them aside with her panties, Becky straddled his naked back. She reached up and speared her fingers through his short crop of hair and massaged his scalp, rubbing at his temples, pressing her thumbs against his neck until she heard the first sigh of contentment.

She continued the massage down his back, over his shoulders and down his arms. She worked each hand until he dropped them limply at his side. Becky moved lower, kneading the bigger muscles of his thighs and buttocks, his calves, his feet. "Oh, God, that's good, darlin'."

"When I want you to talk, I'll ask you to talk." She grinned behind his back. Then she went back to the beginning and skimmed her tiring hands over every inch of him, following each touch with a kiss or a taste. Something clenched here, a muscle quivered there. His breathing grew noisy and erratic, but he held himself still beneath the onslaught of tender, erotic affection.

Becky discovered new ways to tantalize her own sensitized nerves without relying on his touch or husky words. His clean, earthy scent intensified the more she caressed. She lapped the salt from his skin and reveled in the heat of his body. His moans were deep in pitch and vibrated the responsive tips of her breasts as she bent over him. She was breathing harder herself, and drumbeats of anticipation throbbed in her veins. She was slick inside. Swollen and feverish. But still she denied herself the easy completion she knew he'd offer. She wanted him just as hot, just as helpless in his desire for her as she was for him.

Her breasts flattened against his back as she leaned up to his ear and whispered. "Spread yourself a little wider for me."

"Beck—"

"Do it."

He opened his thighs, spreading her legs apart at the same time. She stifled a gasping response in her throat as she opened, fighting the urge to shift and squeeze her own satisfaction from around his thigh as she had that day in the elevator.

But no, she wanted this a certain way. She wanted

to come with him inside her. But she wasn't done with her massage yet.

Feeling her own dampness against her wrist, she reached beneath her, reached between the juncture of his thighs. She fingered his balls gently, then cupped them in her hand, holding on and squeezing lightly as he jerked.

"Oh, God." He groaned, fisting his hands into the pillows as she massaged him there. "No more. Please. No—"

"Roll over."

His hard thighs and crisp hair abraded her clitoris in an unexpected rough caress as he flipped beneath her. Becky caught her lip between her teeth and breathed through the bullet of pleasure that shot to her core. Not yet. Not quite yet.

His beautiful arousal jutted to attention and bobbed before her. He was thick and dark with engorged desire.

She sat back with a smile and looked her fill of that, too. "Becky…" he groaned.

"Shh." She caressed his erection, stroking it from base to tip, tracing its purplish head until that first drop of pre-come glistened at the tip.

"Ah, geez." His hands fisted in the covers.

Becky watched the play of muscles straining from jaw to chest to cock. "Look at me."

Though he gritted his teeth, he opened his eyes and watched her bow down to taste him. She licked away the salty drop. His chest lurched with a deep, quick breath. She swirled her tongue around the tip. He tilted his head back and moaned. She bent down lower, opening her throat and taking as much of him in as she could. Skimming over his groin muscles, she squeezed her hand at the base. She licked him like a lollipop, only his unique taste was strictly adult candy.

He groaned and writhed beneath her feast, and when she sensed that he was about to explode, Becky sat up and straddled him. She captured him between her slick, swollen lips and lowered herself down until he pressed against her deep inside.

He moved his hands to her thighs and gripped them hard. "Darlin', there's no protection…."

"Shh." She braced one hand on his chest and silenced his lips with the other. Her voice came out as husky and uneven as his. "You said anything I want."

"Anything."

She showed him an equal amount of trust by taking him inside her, raw and natural. But she was on the pill, they were both healthy, and he felt oh, so good, hot and pulsing inside her, filling her up.

"Command me," he begged, his mouth a wet kiss against her fingertips, his hips shaking with the effort to keep still beneath her.

"Touch my breasts," she ordered.

His big hands were there at once, cupping the full, heavy globes, lifting, squeezing. He flicked his thumbs over the tips and she threw back her head, stretching her body out to combat the shards of rapture arrowing through each peak and striking deep inside her throbbing center.

Becky pushed herself up slightly with her knees

and began to move, sliding up and down his shaft, sinking lower, squeezing tighter each time.

"Harder," she ordered, closing her eyes and sliding faster. He pinched the pebbled tips between his thumb and fingers. Pleasure hummed in her throat. "Sit up."

He did. Becky rocked back onto his thighs, keeping him sheathed inside her.

"Taste them."

With his hands beneath her bottom, he held her impaled on his lap as he laved his rough tongue around one nipple and then the other.

"More." She clutched his head against her as he nipped at the straining tip. "More," she breathed. His mouth closed wet and hot against her. He suckled, drawing a spike of electricity straight from her womb. His hips bucked beneath her as he neared the brink of his control. "No. Not yet." Shafts of heat swirled up into her brain, out into her fingers, down to her toes.

"Damn it, woman…."

"Now!"

Zachariah thrust his hips hard and pumped himself inside her. She angled his mouth up to hers and screamed her release into his mouth as he devoured her rapture with his kiss.

ZACHARIAH PULLED THE SHEET and coverlet up over their bodies when he felt the first prickle of goose bumps dot Becky's back. The fever had been slow to leave his body, too.

He'd never forget the glorious sight of her lush, pale breasts bobbing above him, their rosy tips dark and hard with her desire. He'd never forget the slick feel of her hot center, pulsing around him, squeezing him with her body and milking every last ounce of pleasure from him until he was exhausted, sated and lying there with her naked and damp, snuggled against his side. But now that they'd had a chance to doze and recover their senses, he lay awake in the darkness, staring into the shadows without seeing any familiar demons there.

He wasn't so idealistic to think that one forbidden night inside the healing haven of Becky's decadent body would cure his battle fatigue and chase away the nightmares forever. But putting himself into her hands and having quite possibly the most incredible sex of his life went a long way toward restoring other parts of him that had been wounded and forgotten.

There was no question in his mind now that he had married Beckster for the right reason. He loved her. The passion they shared was a bonus, but he loved her all the same. Whatever doubts he might have concocted after so many months apart—that their magic had been a fluke of timing, that a Nebraska farm boy and East Coast heiress had little in common to sustain a relationship outside the bedroom, that she wasn't mentally or emotionally equipped to deal with life as a military wife—had been laid to rest tonight.

Part of Zachariah still needed to hear her claim him as her husband, to validate that she was just as committed to him and a future together as he was to her. But he was beginning to realize that coming home after being away for so long and missing so much of each other's lives required time to adjust. Time to get reacquainted. Time—and patience—to discover the changes that had occurred while apart, and to learn to accept and deal with those changes.

While he'd blamed her for keeping secrets and telling lies, he'd been keeping the biggest one of all— the gulf between them since his return was his fault as much as hers.

What reason had he given her to believe in them?

No ring or other tangible sign of his commitment to her.

Brief, sporadic communication.

No consideration of her ignorance regarding deployment. No address to send a care package to. No phone call on their anniversary or her birthday. Hell, he didn't even know when her birthday was.

Demanding that she go public with the news of their hasty wedding without fully understanding the heavy responsibilities she'd been shouldering on her own for such a long time had been asking too much.

Zachariah trailed his fingers up and down Becky's spine as she snored softly against his shoulder. Tough as she was, in some ways she was more vulnerable than any woman he'd ever met. He knew that because the more he got to know her, the more he realized she was a lot like him.

It was his job to protect. It was his calling in life. Just as it was Becky's calling. She didn't carry a gun. She wasn't trained in multiple disarmament procedures or hand-to-hand combat. But she was a warrior all the same. Dimitra Cunningham had needed her, and just as Zachariah reported for duty when he was called to serve, Becky had risked her life against a violent man to fight for her client's rights to a secure, peaceful life.

And while she was taking a stand and being so brave and taking care of others—who was taking care of her for eighteen months? No one.

He wouldn't quit the Corps so he could be with her 24/7, three-hundred-and-sixty-five days a year. But things were going to change. He knew how to be a Marine. Now he vowed to learn how to be a husband, too—even from thousands of miles away.

Her fingers drew a circle across his chest and he smiled.

"You're thinking awfully loudly up there."

"Good thoughts." He hugged her close and kissed the crown of her hair before resuming his leisurely scrolling against her back. This was bliss. This was nirvana.

This was peace.

"Tell me about Watson."

His gut clenched at the mention of the corporal's name. It was still a hard topic to discuss. But the crushing guilt and impotent rage that usually consumed him had mellowed into sorrow.

Maybe he could talk about this now. He had turned all his trust over to Becky physically. Was it possible he could trust her with this, too?

"How do you know about Corporal Watson?"

"You mentioned that you'd lost a man. That you felt responsible for his death. I heard you call his name tonight."

"He was a lance corporal in our unit. He died."

"There's more to it than that."

"He was a good kid. His mother would have been proud of him. I am."

She pressed a soft kiss to his chest. "Did he die in the same explosion where you were hurt?"

"Yeah."

"You need to talk about this. If not with me, then with someone who can help. A therapist. I'm not an expert, but I'm sure you're dealing with post-traumatic stress disorder."

"I am." The major who'd analyzed him had said that he suspected Zachariah was dealing with survivor's guilt and a mixed-up father-son complex—more than the average officer-enlisted man relationship—probably because Darrell Watson had reminded him of his younger brother, which had made him extremely protective of and overly attached to the kid. It might be difficult, but with Becky by his side, he believed he could find a way to deal with his guilt and grief. Learning to cope and moving forward with his life would be a better way to honor his fallen comrade than to stew in the nightmares of the past. "I've had a few conversations with a psychologist back at the base."

"Go back and talk to him some more. It frightens me when you go to that dark place inside your head."

Zachariah laughed. "You're kidding. There's something in this world that scares you?"

He was teasing, but she was not. "There's plenty in this world that scares me, Zachariah. Losing my mother to cancer. Disappointing my ambitious, loving parents who expect so much from me and for me. Knowing there are men out there in the world who hold women hostage in their own homes." She burrowed even closer. "I'm scared that I've done irreparable damage to what you and I had together."

"Let's stay in the moment, darlin'. No regrets. No askin' for trouble. Let's just stay in the moment."

"That's not realistic, though, is it? People change and grow. Our worlds change around us. We have to evolve accordingly or..."

"Or we grow apart." She wanted to know how he'd changed? "I relive Darrell Watson's senseless death every night in my dreams. I guess that bomb today triggered something. It was worse than ever tonight."

"How so?"

"I didn't just lose Watson. I lost you." An image of her death tried to claw its way into Zachariah's mind again. But he fought it back. "It tears me up inside to think I might not have you in my life anymore."

She propped herself up on her elbow and looked down into his face. "You haven't lost me. Do you feel me, Zachariah? I'm right here. I'm real and I'm alive and I'm right here."

He tunneled his fingers into her hair. Those deep blue eyes promised so much and he tried to believe. "I know. But there are other ways to lose you."

"Not tonight."

When she leaned in to kiss him, Zachariah met her halfway. Then he rolled her onto her back and proceeded to seduce her with the same care and tenderness with which she'd seduced her way into his heart.

"LA-DA, LA-DA, LA…SHIT." The familiar Strauss waltz twanged to a stop inside his head as he twisted the last two wires together and capped them off before he accidentally crossed them.

He wiped the sweat off his forehead with the back of his hand, hating that that ice queen of an attorney was such kindling for his temper. His nostrils flared as he breathed in deeply and focused on the supposedly soothing orchestral music playing on his stereo. A vivid image of Becky Owens screaming in pain, begging him for mercy, blotted out the next step of the assembly process in his brain.

Not yet.

But soon. Very soon.

Screw her for messing with his head. *Screw her.*

He was in control. He was the man.

She was nobody.

Or she damn straight was going to feel like a nobody by the time he was done with her.

A familiar hum of power swept through his blood and evened out his pulse.

"That's right, bitch. You're nobody."

Sure of himself once more, he slid the entire trigger assembly into its casing with careful precision, smiling once the mechanism clicked into place. "Nicely done."

Of course, it was. He was good at what he did. He'd learned to work with his hands long before he'd discovered his full potential. He was a man with a destiny.

And she thought she could deny him that destiny? "Not this time."

He picked up a cell phone from his workbench, dialed

the number and waited. A few seconds later, the mechanism's red light blinked on and he smiled at his success.

Tomorrow night he'd be free and unfettered by Becky Owens's emasculating control over his life.

Tomorrow night, she'd bow down to his power. He'd strip every arrogant cell off the bitch's icy hide. She'd know her place before she gave him everything he deserved.

He reset the trigger, then placed it in his briefcase beside the pristine white envelope and the last two bricks of C-4 explosive his contact had misappropriated from the Matalin demolition site. Then he closed and locked the aluminum case. He dropped the phone into the pocket of his tuxedo jacket and stood and stretched.

He plucked down her picture from over his workbench and caressed the unflattering shot of her sprawling on the pavement in the courthouse parking lot. The brilliant shine of her hair was dulled by grime. Her leg and hands were bloodied, her expression dazed and afraid.

She looked weak, vulnerable. He loved it.

A familiar power waltzed through his veins as he stroked the photo of her pale, fear-lined face. "If I'd wanted you dead yesterday, you'd be dead. But I'm a reasonable man. I'll give you one more chance to make things right." He pulled a craft knife from his toolbox and set the photograph down on the workbench to carve the hulking Goliath out of the picture. "Dance with me, Miss Owens."

He cradled the photo in his hands and danced in the

empty half of the garage beside the tan SUV he'd rented. "La-da, la-da, da-da…"

After blowing up her car, she would take him more seriously. She couldn't get away with treating him the way she did. Like she was better than him. Like he wasn't a real man.

Tomorrow night, he'd make her understand that living or dying was her choice. Give him what he wanted and live. Or…

He kissed her picture, then crumpled it in his fist. "Die."

12

THE FOLLOWING MORNING, Zachariah held out his mug for Lily Owens to top off his coffee. When she offered him the plate of Danish rolls, he had to hold up his hand to refuse any more food.

"No, thanks. I know it looks like I'll hold a lot, but even with my size, there's a limit."

Lily laughed as she set the coffeepot on their breakfast tray. "Your mother must have fed you well to grow you that big."

Zachariah nodded. "Yeah, she'd give Delia a run for her money." He was looking forward to his flight to Nebraska on Monday to see his family. He just hoped he wouldn't be flying alone.

Lily unwrapped an armful of fresh-cut flowers Frederick had brought to the table earlier. "How did you sleep last night?"

With a busty blonde and a hard-on? Zachariah quickly took a drink to hide his wicked grin. Yeah, like he'd share that tidbit with this gentle woman who didn't know she was his mother-in-law.

He opted for a bit of selective honesty. "My shoulder's still a little stiff. But my dreams have been sweet and I haven't been tossin' and turnin' as much as I sometimes do."

"I'm glad to hear that."

Over Becky's protests, Zachariah had been up front with her parents about the car bomb—as much to make them aware of their own need to be cautious as to spare his conscience of any more lies. Though he'd avoided mentioning how long the threats had been going on and that the explosion was a culmination, not a one-time thing, he knew they wouldn't be able to fool Lily for long. He was quickly learning that she was far too intuitive for them to get away with pretending nothing at all had happened. She'd notice Becky's scraped leg and bruises—and the stiff way he'd been carrying himself after their hard landing on the unforgiving concrete. Leaving her in the dark would only worry her more.

Lily trimmed another sprig of the columbine flowers she was arranging in a vase. She set her shears down with a heavy sigh. "Frightening what the world is coming to. It's like when Becky was a little girl and I'd just found out Bertram and I wouldn't be able to have more children. I'm almost afraid to let her out the door. Or to let anyone else in."

Zachariah touched her wrist in reassurance. "Richmond PD has filed formal charges against Nick Cunningham. He may be out on bail, but Chief Wesley assured me he'll have an officer watching him round the clock. Plus, my team and I will be working the party tonight, along with Senator Barclay's security contingent. I promise you, Cunningham won't get close to your daughter again. Or any of you. I'll keep Becky safe. I promise."

Lily patted his hand and smiled. "You're such a dear young man. I know we're well protected with you here. Goodness knows you watch over my daughter like a guard dog. I'm sure you're the most devoted security man we've ever hired."

Um, yeah. About that…Hell, if Lily hadn't already guessed the depth of his feelings, she'd certainly be able to intuit that he and Becky were, at the very least, attracted to each other. If he could lead men into enemy territory and hold his own in an argument with Becky Owens, then he should have the guts to face this petite slip of a woman. "Lily, would you change your opinion of me—I mean, would it be totally off the wall or unacceptable if…I asked your daughter to go out with me sometime?"

She pushed the flowers aside and turned in her chair. At the arch of her snowy-white eyebrow, Zachariah sat up straighter, wondering if he'd misjudged their early mornings together. He'd thought a bond had formed between them, but maybe their daily breakfasts had been more about a lonely woman seeking companionship—even with the hired help if he was the only one available—rather than a real friendship.

But the Owens women always surprised him. "Thank God one of you finally said something." She swatted his arm as though he'd been a dolt for not presenting the idea sooner. "I wondered when you were going to get around to that."

"You noticed?"

"That you have feelings for her? Becky is smart and beautiful and has an attitude tough enough to go head-to-head with you. How could you resist that?"

Zachariah didn't know whether to hug the woman or be very, very scared that she always seemed to know what was going on, no matter how her family tried to shelter her. He hastened to reassure her that following his heart didn't mean he'd be neglecting his job here. "Becky's safety still comes first. I won't do anything to compromise that, I promise." He narrowed his eyes and studied her as she resumed her work on the bouquet. "How did you know?"

"You are many things, Mr. Clark, but a good actor is not one of them. I've seen the looks you give her. Whether annoyed or concerned or…interested—just the fact that you're looking so much is a dead giveaway. And I know my daughter. She's picky. Has high standards for herself and the people she cares about. No matter what she says or how she acts—which has been a little erratic lately, mind you, so I can tell something's up—she's giving you those same looks back. Ergo, there's something going on between you. Something fairly serious if I'm any judge of character."

"Ergo, eh?" He could strike one worry off his list. News of a marriage itself might still be a shocker, but knowing *he* was the son-in-law wouldn't be. "You're one sharp cookie, aren't you, Lil'?"

Lily smiled and he could see why Bertram Owens had fallen in love with her—why he was still in love with her after thirty years of marriage. *He* hoped to be so lucky. "I was sick, Zachariah. But I was never stupid."

"No, ma'am." He couldn't help grinning as he pushed back his chair and stood. "Well, I'd best get to work. Lots of things I need to double-check before the party tonight."

On impulse, he bent down and kissed her cheek. She touched the spot as it bloomed with color. "Heavens."

"Thanks, Lily."

Zachariah headed for the door, but paused as another impulsive thought hit. "Oh, and could you recommend a good jewelry store in Richmond?"

"FINALLY, I'D LIKE TO THANK our hosts—Bertram and Lily Owens, and their daughter, Becky. What a delightful repast and what an auspicious gathering of knowledgeable, civic-minded friends. Without people like them, we couldn't make the important things happen in Washington. I thank you all. And don't forget to vote." Ralph Barclay finished his obligatory speech to a noisy mix of laughter and applause, then descended the staircase to start shaking hands with the guests who'd backed up their verbal support with the thousands of dollars raised tonight.

Becky stood at the back of the crowded entryway near the front door, and wondered how rude it would be for the hostess he'd just thanked to slip outside and run away like Cinderella from the ball. She'd be happy to toss both her slippers—the strappy high-heels weren't meant for four hours of mingling and dancing. And the noise level of more than one hundred people talking all at once had already wormed its way into her skull to give her the beginnings of a headache.

She inched toward the door. Maybe five minutes of

fresh air was all she needed. And if she kicked off her shoes and kept on running…? Well, her job was done here, right?

"I know what you're thinking." Zachariah's deep voice sounded like a whisper beneath the crowd noise. She looked across to the other side of the door where he was standing guard. Clad in an ordinary black tuxedo and crisp white shirt that looked anything but ordinary on his big frame, he was definitely the most stunning decoration around the house tonight. The earpiece he wore, wire curling down beneath his collar, the bulge of the gun holstered at his back and the stone-faced alertness of his expression, should have been more of a deterrent to her stealing glances at him from across the room all night. "You'd like to ditch this shindig."

She turned her focus back to the milling crowd. "Wanna come with me?"

"I'm workin', Miss Owens. I don't know if the lady who hired me would think too highly of me runnin' away before the party's over."

"What if the lady who hired you ordered you to run away?"

"Well, I don't mind takin' orders from her…in the right setting."

She shrugged, shifting the satin strap of the ice-blue gown she wore off one shoulder. She let him get a glance of the bare skin there before sliding it back into place. "The dance floor isn't the right setting? The chamber orchestra will start playing again in the ballroom now that the speeches are done."

"I was thinkin' more along the lines of one of the

upstairs bedrooms. Or the cab of my truck. *If* my boss ordered me to."

Becky finally turned to him and smiled. "Well, she might…"

"You have them eating out of the palm of your hand, Senator." James Enderle, the senator's campaign manager, had steered the senator to a few key support- ers in attendance. And now, just as the party was finally starting to get interesting for her, James cupped her elbow and turned Becky for the senator to shake her hand. "Ralph, this is the little lady you'll want to thank."

She tried to pay more attention to the senator's sincere thanks than to the hand that continued to rest at the small of her back as though it belonged there. Zachariah had been sweetly jealous of James's hands- on approach to a conversation, but now she was begin- ning to get a little annoyed herself. She had no problem with a friend touching her, but there'd been something almost possessive about James's attention to her tonight. True, they'd worked side by side to make this reception happen, but the party was winding down now. James could take his hands and go hit on one of the eligible women in attendance.

"You're most welcome, Senator." Becky accepted his thanks, then stepped away from James to search out her mother. Once she spotted Lily Owens holding court in the sitting room, Becky linked her arm through the senator's and escorted him in. "My mother's the real inspiration behind all this hard work, Senator Barclay. I know she'd enjoy the opportunity to chat with you for a few minutes."

"I'd love to." The senator thanked her again, then shooed away James, who'd followed them. "James, you go enjoy the party. After I speak to Lily, I'll head on back to my hotel. You and I can debrief in the morning."

"Yes, sir. I'll see you then."

When the senator left the conversation, Becky hoped to do the same. But she hadn't taken a step before James took her hand and linked her arm through his. "Let's dance."

Sure. What was one more dance when her toes were already going numb? "I'd rather not. My feet—"

"Even better. Let's go find someplace quiet to have a chat and catch up. I'd like to talk to you about another event you might like to host."

She laughed. "Oh, no. Once every six years is plenty often for me."

"I'm not talking about Ralph Barclay's campaign." They'd moved beyond the dining room and ballroom and ended up at the black doors leading to her father's study. James opened one for her. "Tonight was a terrific success, Becky. You're a natural at this."

While he closed the door behind him and shut out the noise from the party, Becky took a moment to plop onto one of the leather sofas and simply soak up the blessed silence. "Oh, I can still hear the pounding in my ears." She bent down to unbuckle her shoes and pull them off her feet. "I'll never get those back on, but who cares? The party's winding down, right?"

She gently massaged around the scab on her ankle, completely absorbed for the moment in getting comfortable and finally getting the strain of this week over with. Until she heard the clink of ice in a glass and looked over to see James at her father's bar, pouring two drinks.

"Make yourself at home," she teased, though she was more annoyed than amused at the liberty he'd taken. When he offered a bourbon to her, she shook her head. "No thanks. I already have a headache coming on. That'd be the last thing I need." Becky closed her eyes and leaned back on the couch. "If you're looking to do something else like this for Senator Barclay, count me out. Don't get me wrong—I intend to vote for the man, but this just isn't…"

The leather creaked beside her on the couch, startling her eyes open the instant before James's thigh bumped against hers. She scooted over another couple of inches to give him the room he needed.

"Ralph Barclay is not the only great leader our country has, Becky." It sounded like a formal announcement.

"Senator Barclay is Mom's pet project. But between my work and her health, I don't think we can fundraise for any other candidates right now."

"The Owens name is synonymous with successful politicians in both Richmond and Washington, D.C. You can't ignore your birthright."

James slid closer until his leg touched hers again. Not by accident, not when he'd cornered her at the arm of the couch like this. *Give it up, already,* she wanted to say. Her old friend was no different than her mother or father or even her—he had a cause that inspired him. She couldn't fault him for being as enthusiastic about his work as she was about hers, so instead of calling him on the touchy-feely thing, she took a polite out and pushed to her feet. There were two couches in the study, and any of a dozen rooms in the house she could move to if she wanted her space.

"One day, the name James Enderle will be just as big, just as influential, I'm sure." If he wanted a few strokes to his ego, she could concede that. "Maybe even more so." She bent down to scoop up her shoes. "I wish you all the luck in the world, James. Thanks for the break. But I'd better get back on duty."

She crossed to the door and opened it. She'd have never suspected James could move so fast, but when she would have stepped out into the hallway, an arm reached over her shoulder and slammed the door shut from behind her.

Decorum be damned. Becky whirled around. "What the hell are you doing?"

"I'm having a conversation here. And I expect you to listen."

The grinding clench of his jaw as he spoke was neither friendly nor decorous.

Becky raised a distancing hand. "I've had enough politics for one evening. I'm saying good-night to my parents and I'm heading to bed."

She turned to leave.

James's fingers dug into her arm as he swung her around and shoved her against the door.

"What are you—"

"You have to learn to respect me, Becky."

"I used to." She wedged her hands between them

and tried to push him away. "Have you gone nuts? Let go of me."

He leaned in farther, locking the door behind her and rendering her hands useless though she continued to struggle. "Why did you break up with me? Why didn't you marry me?"

What? "You never asked."

"I'm asking you now, bitch." *Oh. My. God.* Becky went still. She nearly blacked out as the blood in her head drained to her toes. Her wobbly knees might have collapsed if James hadn't wedged her so tightly against the door. She could only stare at the thin, articulate lips, spitting what should have been a romantic request in her face. "We are supposed to be together. The Enderles and the Owenses. It's our destiny."

Finally remembering to breathe, Becky tried to think, tried to reason. But all that came out was, "James—we were friends. What have you done?"

He snatched her by the wrist and slung her back onto the sofa hard enough that the furniture moved. She felt the sting on her leg as a wound reopened, but ignored the pain and scrambled to her feet. But she had nowhere to go. James had advanced, forcing her to retreat.

"There's another bomb, Becky. Right here at the party." He pulled a cell phone from the pocket of his tux and held it up beside his cold blue eyes. "When I said I intended to create a little drama tonight, I wasn't kidding. All I have to do is dial a number and the countdown begins."

"You can't blackmail me into marrying you."

"You're not listening to me! Don't you understand?

I'm the one with the power here." He tapped the phone against his temple and took a deep breath to calm himself—as though suave and articulate insanity was an improvement over his temperamental outburst. "If you weren't such a frigging uptight bitch we could have done this the easy way. But I wasn't good enough for you. You just wanted to be friends, you said. Don't you understand? You can't treat a man that way. You can't interfere with the natural order of things. I slept with you so that you'd marry me. I didn't want to, but that's the way it's supposed to be between us."

"No." Becky reached behind her, knocking papers and knickknacks off the desk as she tried to find something to arm herself with. All she found was the chair. She moved it between them as he circled the desk. "James. You need help."

"Don't say that!" He picked up the chair and hurled it across the room.

Terrified by his unexpected strength, Becky screamed and ran. "Zachariah! Zacha—"

James tackled her from behind, knocking her down to the rug. She kicked, clawed, hit. And when his wrist came within reach of her teeth, she bit.

"You bitch!" He cursed and rolled away, cradling his wounded arm.

"Zachariah!" She tripped over the long hem of her dress as she tried to stand.

It was all the advantage James needed to seize her wrist and wrench her to her feet. He clutched the phone in his other hand, waved it in her face. "I'll do this, Becky. Don't think I won't. That bruiser who follows you around like a puppy will die. Your mother. Your father. A national senator. All dead. All on your head."

"No!"

"Come with me now or I'll make this pretty life of yours all go away." He punched in a number.

"No!" She reached for the phone but he held it easily beyond her reach. *Reason with him!* "I mean—why don't we go dance and discuss it? We can announce our engagement at the party tonight." She attempted a shaky smile.

"That's not good enough. Don't you understand about destiny? Your father and mine met and became friends for a reason. We're like Romeo and Juliet. Think of everything we could accomplish if our two families were joined. You and I could go all the way to the White House one day."

Romeo and Juliet died. "Don't do this, James."

"Becky!" Her name roared from the other side of the door. *Zachariah. Safety. Hope.*

James punched in the second number.

"Are you crazy?" she yelled.

"Becky! Get away from the door!"

She jerked against the vise of James's hand and dropped, knocking them both off balance and tumbling to the floor. "We're clear!"

"I'm dialing." James pressed the third, the fourth.

Becky jumped at the two rapid explosions outside the door. Not big booms. Gunshots.

She scrambled for the cell phone, but James was stronger.

"I'm already married, you fruitcake!" she shouted,

desperate to stop him from completing that call. She kicked him, but her bare feet were useless. "I am Mrs. Zachariah Clark. I have a husband!"

The door burst open. Big hands closed around Becky's shoulders and pulled her to her feet. "Are you all right?"

"Yes, but—"

The same hands pushed her behind the wall of black tuxedos. Deke and Murphy. Zachariah leveled his gun at James.

"No!" She fought to get around them. Time was running out. "He has a bomb! He's dialing the trigger!"

Zachariah punched James square in the jaw and knocked him out cold. He picked up the phone from the crumpled madman and turned to his men. "Clear the house. Now."

THE MOONLIGHT COULDN'T COMPETE with the spinning red, white and blue lights of a dozen police cars. Like the facade of a surreal disco, the Owens house was captured in an eerie glare of spotlights and the strobe effect of cars from the police, Secret Service and FBI.

But Becky barely saw any of that.

Even knowing a groggy James Enderle was just a few yards away from her, handcuffed in the back of one of the police cars, wasn't enough to distract her from watching Marine Corps Captain Zachariah Clark in action.

She stood off to the side with her parents and the remaining guests out beyond the front drive's security gate, wrapped in blankets from EMTs, and looking like a band of refugees from some high society war zone. She watched as her bodyguard donned a flak vest and tool belt and grabbed a helmet from the back of a TAC team truck. With precise, methodical movements and clipped orders, he was turning Deke, Murphy and a team of police officers into his own private army.

He gave a command to Police Chief Wesley. "Turn off all cell phones. Sir, I'd like you and your men to collect every phone, BlackBerry, pager, anything electronic, just in case it can be triggered by another number or any random satellite signal."

The older man left to do Zachariah's bidding. Other men were sent out to search the grounds. He told Deke and Murphy they would follow some plan called "Sunshine Halo" and they nodded as though it made sense.

But even if she didn't understand the lingo, she understood the actions. They were going into that house where James had put a bomb. They were going to search it from attic to wine cellar to make sure there was nothing else remotely insane that James might have planted on the premises.

And Zachariah was going to take that bomb apart.

"All right, men. Helmets on. Move out."

"Yes, sir."

"No." Hurrying beyond the clutch of her father's hand, Becky shed her blanket and ran after him. "Zachariah!"

He nodded to the officer who tried to stop her, and once free to approach, she ducked beneath the yellow Crime Scene ribbon, hiked up her dress and ran barefoot across the grass to meet her husband. She didn't stop until she could wrap her arms around his waist and hold him tight, burying her cheek against the slick nylon shell of his vest. "You can't do this. It's too dangerous."

He dropped the helmet at his feet and folded his arms around her. "This is what I do for a living, darlin'. I have to go in."

She leaned back against his arms. "What if you have another flashback while you're in there? What if you forget where you are and what you're doing and you make a mistake?"

He kissed her on the top of her head and released her. "I won't."

When he picked up his helmet and started to move away, she stopped him again. He had to listen to reason. "Zachariah Clark, I love you. I don't want to lose you."

"Did I stop you from doing your job when that pretty boy bastard was sending you threats and making calls? Did I keep you from protecting Dimitra Cunningham?"

"No, but—"

"Then you can't keep me from this." He hunkered down to her level and looked her straight in the eye. "Don't you think I was scared to death when you were stubborn enough to go to work every day—to face that abuser in court—to let you out of your apartment to risk your life for someone else?"

"I know you were. But that's different."

He straightened proudly, towering over. "The uniform's different—you wear a suit, I wear fatigues. But I had to trust that you were smart, you were well trained, you took the precautions you needed to—and then I had to let you go do your job." He reached out to brush aside a tendril of hair the breeze had swept across her cheek. "You need to do the same for me. Trust me that I'm just doin' the job I need to do."

Becky held on to his wrist and leaned into the tender caress. "But I had you to protect me. You were always there to watch my back."

He nodded to Deke and Murphy. "What do you think I keep these two yahoos around for?" He tucked her under the crook of his arm and turned to his men. "Head out. I want a top-to-bottom sweep. When we spot the device, you do not—I repeat, do not—try to disarm that thing until I get there."

"Yes, sir." Deke, looking all business, nodded and was off.

Murphy grinned around Zachariah's shoulder. "He keeps me around because I'm so good-lookin'."

Zachariah put his hand in the middle of Murphy's face and shoved the flirt away.

But as Murphy jogged on up to catch his buddy and enter the house, Becky wasn't laughing. She could see the logic of Zachariah's argument, but something very illogical kept her arms wrapped tightly around him.

"I know you have to do this, but it's a bomb, damn it. And James clearly isn't thinking with a full deck. There could be something else in there, and you won't know where it is."

"Like the enemy at night?"

"Not funny, big guy."

"Here." Zachariah pried himself free. He pulled a

small box from his pocket and put it in her hand, wrapping her fingers around it. "You hold on to this until I get back. Don't open it. Not until I'm with you to do it proper." She nodded and clutched it tightly, caring less about the gift than the man. "And by the way, the next time you want to shout to the whole world that you're my wife, let's do it in a church."

He leaned down and kissed her hard and quick.

Her mother and father had come to stand with her by the time he'd strapped on his helmet and disappeared into the house.

Only then did Becky look at the gift in her hand.

It was a ring box.

SHE'D CALLED HERSELF *Mrs. Zachariah Clark.* Shouted it to that whack-job Enderle like it was a name to be proud of. Like it fit. Like she was all his and nobody, not even a man with a bomb, could make her say any different.

He shouldn't be thinking about that right now. Not while he still carried the disassembled firing mechanism in his hand. Not when he should be giving a situation report to Police Chief Wesley. The threat had been neutralized. They'd found the bomb in one of the bathrooms. Zachariah's hands had been steady and his mind clear as he took the bomb apart. The Owenses and their guests were safe. The senator was safe.

Becky was safe.

Mrs. Zachariah Clark.

He couldn't stop grinning.

A man of duty, he did stop to brief Chief Wesley and informed the TAC unit—minus Nick Cunningham, thank you very much—of the bomb's location so they could safely remove the C-4.

Then he started walking.

He tossed the helmet, lost the toolbelt and stripped off the vest, never breaking stride as he crossed the police barrier and headed for his wife. People thanked him and patted his back and moved aside, respecting the walk, respecting a man on a mission.

He marched right up to Becky Owens-Clark, dusted the blanket off her shoulders, picked her up and kissed her. Deeply. Tenderly. Thoroughly. He savored her weight in his arms, her breasts against his chest, the hum in her throat and the clutch of her hands around his neck.

His blood was pumping strong and fast when he finally set her on her feet and went down on one knee in front of her.

"I'm doing it right this time." He took her hand, wrapped both his big ones around hers and the box she held. He tipped his face up to those beautiful blue eyes. "Becky Owens. I love you. You know how much I want your body, but I *need* your heart. I want it with me, every day of my life, no matter where I am in this world. I need you. So, before anything else happens that can keep us apart, will you marry me? Again?"

Oh, damn.

That pouty mouth trembled with a crooked smile and tears welled up in her eyes. She'd faced down a whiny attorney, an abusive ex-husband and a pretty boy with a bomb fetish and hadn't batted an eye. She'd argued with him, done battle with his nightmares and loved him out of his mind. Without shedding a single tear. She was one tough chick.

"So *now* you're crying?"

There was a gentle nudge at Becky's back. "She says 'yes,'" Lily shouted. "Again."

Becky laughed and fell into his arms. "I'd marry you any day. Anywhere. As many times as you want, big guy. There's no logic to it, but my heart is yours. It always has been. I love you."

"I love you back."

He kissed her good, hugged her tight and fantasized about all the ways they were gonna celebrate this perfect moment. He pulled them both to their feet, pulled the diamond solitaire from its box. He paused a moment before slipping it onto her finger.

"Say it," he commanded.

Becky grinned. "Yes."

They got more applause than the senator's speech.

And as his soon-to-be-wife-again grabbed his collar and pulled him down for a kiss to reseal the deal, Zachariah saw Bertram lean over and whisper to Lily. "What did you mean—again? Did I miss something?"

Lily curled her arm through his and gave Zachariah a wink. "I'll explain it to you later, dear."

Epilogue

"RUN, DARLIN'. I'M DOWN TO fifteen minutes."

Becky held on to Zachariah's hand and hurried her steps into double time to keep up with her husband's long strides across the parking lot. A task made extra difficult by her efforts to rebutton her blouse as they ran.

But she was laughing. "Well, hell, if I'd known you had that much time left on your leave, we could have spent another five minutes in your truck."

"Careful, Beckster," he growled with a promise. "Or I will do you right here up against the barracks wall where God and anybody walkin' by can see."

"O-oh. Sex in public. We haven't tried that one yet."

He nearly stumbled as he stopped with a groan. He caught her up in his arms and kissed her before resting his forehead against hers. "And here I thought three months was a short deployment."

She curled her fingers into his collar. "They're going to be the longest three months of my life until I see you again."

"Me, too. I'll e-mail you as soon as I can. And I'll call and talk about Travis's offer to work with him here at Quantico training the new recruits."

Becky nodded, knowing he was still torn about giving up his Special Ops assignment and taking a stateside job. But they'd discuss it—like they should have discussed the other big decisions and problems they'd faced in their lives. They'd do better this time around. "Sounds like a plan."

He grinned and reached down to refasten the misaligned buttons on her blouse. "Now your mom will see those and know we're runnin' late because I had to have you one more time before the honeymoon was over."

Becky held him close when he would have pulled away. "It's never going to be over for us, big guy. Every time you come home, it'll be like the first time all over again."

"There might be more changes to get used to."

"I know. But we'll have new ideas, too. New things to learn about each other. New ways to make us work."

"Sounds like a plan," he agreed. He winked and grabbed her hand. "Let's go." He pointed to the crowd of people waiting inside the fence up ahead of them. "There are your folks. Hell, they're chattin' up Mom and Dad. Which reminds me, three months from now? Nebraska. Skinny-dipping. You promised."

"In three months it'll be fall. The water will be cold."

"We get a lot of Indian summers during harvest time. And if the weather is cold, you'll just have to cuddle a little closer."

"I was game for that hayloft idea," she countered.

"You'll do both if I know you."

And then there was five minutes of hugging and

tears and shaking hands and hugging some more as Zachariah said goodbye to his family and to hers.

As Zachariah's commander summoned the unit to line up for checking in and loading up the bus, her new-again husband threw his arm across her shoulders and tucked her to his side.

"Now don't forget about contacting the military support group, darlin'."

"I won't," she reassured him. "Deke's mother is going to call to give me a schedule of the Richmond group's events. Plus, she wants to take Mom and me to lunch so we can get to know each other."

"That's all Lily needs—a new cause."

Becky's mother, looking pink and healthy for this morning's send-off, stepped up to pat Zachariah's chest. "I heard my name. Now don't worry about that wedding reception I'm planning. I promise to keep it as small and tasteful as your ceremony was. I mean the second one, of course. It'll probably be a little fancier than your first effort."

"Yes, ma'am." Lily stretched up on tiptoe, coming nowhere close to reaching Zachariah. So he obliged her by stooping down to kiss her cheek and trade hugs.

"Fall in!"

Their families drifted a few polite feet away as Zachariah turned Becky in his arms. "This is it, darlin'. I'm off again. Be sure you go to the doctor and get that mammogram like we discussed. If breast cancer is a family history thing then I want you to stay on top of it."

"You really love these puppies, don't you?"

"I really love *you*."

Her ring sparkled in the sunlight as she framed Zachariah's face and pulled him down for one last heartfelt kiss. "I love you. Do your job. Do it well. Then come home to me, big guy."

He grinned. "At your command."

MILLS & BOON
Blaze

On sale 3rd July 2009

(2-IN-1 ANTHOLOGY)
**NOBODY DOES IT BETTER
& FULL CIRCLE**
by Jennifer LaBrecque & Shannon Hollis

Nobody Does It Better

Devastatingly hot English spy Gage is on enigmatic Holly's
trail. And he's willing to do anything – including acting out
her most sensual fantasies – to capture her!

Full Circle

Cate needs her rugged ex Daniel's help. Yet when they begin
working together again they soon realise that the molten-hot
attraction they once shared is still sizzling…

HAVE MERCY
by Jo Leigh

Concierge Mercy has seen it all working at the exclusive
Hush Hotel. But when sexy Will saunters in she's shocked
by the fantasies he generates. This is one man who could
unleash the coy beauty's inner bad girl!

JUST TRY ME…
by Jill Shalvis

Adrenaline junkie Lily is no stranger to taking chances…until
an accident nearly took her life. Now her latest job, guiding a
simple hiking trip through the Sierras, hardly qualifies as risky.
Until she meets dangerously gorgeous Jared…

FREE!

2 Books
and a surprise gift!

We would like to take this opportunity to thank you for reading this Mills & Boon® book by offering you the chance to take TWO more specially selected titles from the Blaze® series absolutely FREE! We're also making this offer to introduce you to the benefits of the Mills & Boon® Book Club™—

★ FREE home delivery
★ FREE monthly Newsletter
★ Books available before they're in the shops
★ FREE gifts and competitions
★ Exclusive Book Club offers

Accepting these FREE books and gift places you under no obligation to buy, you may cancel at any time, even after receiving your free shipment. Simply complete your details below and return the entire page to the address below. You don't even need a stamp!

YES! Please send me 2 free Blaze books and a surprise gift. I understand that unless you hear from me, I will receive 3 superb new titles every month, including a 2-in-1 title priced at £4.99 and two single titles priced at £3.19 each. Postage and packing free. I am under no obligation to purchase any books and may cancel my subscription at any time. The free books and gift will be mine to keep in any case.

K9ZEF

Ms/Mrs/Miss/Mr ....Initials ....

Surname ....

Address ....
BLOCK CAPITALS PLEASE

....

....Postcode ....

Send this whole page to:
UK: FREEPOST CN81, Croydon, CR9 3WZ